"Everything that's happened to me isn't worth repeating."

Joel balled his hands and put them in his pockets.

"How come you won't trust me?" Shelby whispered.

"Shelby—believe me when I say I already trust you more than any other person in my life."

"I can only get as close to you as you'll let me."

Precisely the problem. Did he want a close relationship like she did? Sure, he enjoyed spending time with her and she got him to smile like he hadn't in a long time. But were those things worth the pain that more than likely would accompany the moment she decided she was done with him?

Shelby looked as if she was going to start crying again. He had to say something.

He cleared his throat. Why was this so difficult? "I…I don't want you to look at me differently."

"I won't."

"*You will.* Everyone does." They heard about sad little Joel Palermo and they all got the same look. That cartoon-eyes-welling-up-with-tears face. Their expressions a clear mix of wondering if they should hug him or step away slowly.

"Maybe we should go back." Shelby sighed.

He caught her arm. "Stay. Please." Joel's eyes searched hers.

"Give me a reason to stay."

Jessica Keller is a Starbucks drinker, avid reader and chocolate aficionado. Jessica holds degrees in communications and biblical studies. She is multipublished in both romance and young-adult fiction and loves to interact with readers through social media. Jessica lives in the Chicagoland suburbs with her amazing husband, beautiful daughter and two annoyingly outgoing cats who happen to be named after superheroes. Find all her contact information at jessicakellerbooks.com.

Books by Jessica Keller

Love Inspired

Goose Harbor Series

The Widower's Second Chance
The Fireman's Secret

Home for Good

Visit the Author Profile page at Harlequin.com for more titles.

The Fireman's Secret

Jessica Keller

HARLEQUIN® LOVE INSPIRED®

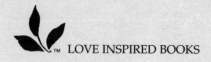

™ LOVE INSPIRED BOOKS

ISBN-13: 978-0-373-87940-3

The Fireman's Secret

Copyright © 2015 by Jessica Koschnitzky

www.Harlequin.com

Printed in U.S.A.

For we are God's handiwork,
created in Christ Jesus to do good works,
which God prepared in advance for us to do.
—*Ephesians* 2:10

For my sweet Anna.
The person God made you to be will always
be enough. Never forget that or allow anyone
to make you feel differently. You are loved
beyond comprehension, just as you are.

Chapter One

Moonlight flashed like a strobe light through the dense canopy of trees lining the road just a mile away from the shores of Lake Michigan. Shelby rolled down her window to let the cool breeze kiss her skin, but the air hung thick with a strong after-rain worm smell and the wind caused the important deed papers sitting on her passenger seat to stir. She promptly rolled the window back up.

Dampness clung to her toes. The running shoes she wore might be ruined now, but dogs needed to be walked and let outside for a little bit, even when it rained.

Her one working headlight bounced off a green sign. Welcome to Goose Harbor. As she read those words, the muscles in her shoulders relaxed instantly. *Home.*

Perhaps she'd drive past the land she'd inherited. Until now, she'd avoided the street the old church had been on—not wanting to see the barren lot or be reminded of the day that had changed her life. The congregation had never rebuilt the church after it burned down, and somehow Shelby felt as if her life hadn't been able to move forward since then. Rebuilding the church wouldn't take away the scars she had received from being trapped in the burning structure all those years ago, but maybe seeing the church standing again would help her move on.

It had to.

A hill came into view and she gunned the car's engine. Bad idea. The vehicle started to shake uncontrollably.

"Please don't die on me," she begged. She eased off the gas and watched the dials on the dashboard bounce. "Please, please, please."

She glanced back at the road and gasped.

A deer leaped onto the street no more than ten feet in front of her. In a split-second calculation, Shelby realized there was no time to move out of the way. She was going too fast. She jammed her foot on the brakes. The car's tires squealed, and like a madman on a warpath, her Volkswagen struck the deer.

Shelby's head lashed forward, slamming against the steering wheel. The car's one good headlight blinked out. The deer flew up onto the hood. White-knuckling the steering wheel, Shelby hung on as her car careered into the steep, wet ditch, tossing gravel and glass shards like candy from a parade float.

With a final death groan, the car came to a rest.

Headlights on the road pulled to a halt above her. A car door slammed.

A deep, male voice called out. "Hello? Are you hurt?" The man skidded down the ditch. He wrenched open her door. "Is it just you in here or are there others?"

"Only me." She coughed and turned a bit, catching a glimpse of his black leather coat.

He stayed her with a hand on her shoulder. "Maybe you shouldn't get up just yet."

The man crouched and his face came into view. Rich hazel eyes full of concern, jaw set, and spiked black hair—he looked as if he belonged on a motorcycle. He couldn't be from Goose Harbor, because she didn't know him—and she knew everyone in her small town.

His dark eyebrows scrunched. "I saw you swerve off the road. Looks like you've got a cut on your forehead. Does anything else hurt?" He tapped his left temple to show her where the cut was.

"I'm okay…I think." Shelby yanked a napkin from her purse and pressed it to her cut. "How's the deer?"

He kept his hand on her shoulder. "Let's worry about you right now. My name's Joel. I'm a fireman, so I'm a trained EMT. I'd like to make sure your head's okay before you get up." His forehead creased as he assessed her. Leaning close, Joel inspected the wound with his warm eyes.

"I'm okay." Shelby tugged at her sleeves, pulling them as low on her wrists as she could. Whoever he was, Joel didn't know about the burn marks on her arms and legs, and she'd like it to stay that way. The less he stared at her, the better.

But he didn't move. "Are you having any feelings of nausea or a quick onset headache?"

"Seriously, I'm fine." She glanced at the napkin she'd been holding to her head. It didn't look like she was bleeding that badly.

"Do me a favor and wait here for a second." The fireman turned and climbed back to his vehicle. A couple of minutes later, he carefully navigated his way back down the slippery slope with a tube of paste, a small flashlight and gauze in his hands.

"Humor me?" He clicked on the flashlight and bent to be eye-level with her. "Okay, I'm going to shine this in your eyes."

Shelby squinted and he told her to keep her eyes open.

"Great." He clicked off the flashlight and tucked it into one of his coat pockets. "Your eyes responded how they should, so that's good news."

"Well, that's a relief." She grinned at him.

"You have pretty eyes." He stopped what he was doing for a moment and his face relaxed—like how she imagined he would have looked at her if their eyes met across a coffee shop. The moment was over too soon. He immediately snapped back into EMT mode.

"Here." He unwrapped the gauze. "We need to put this on your head. It'll work a whole lot better than that napkin."

With two fingers, Joel gently moved her hair out of the way. "I'm going to put some of this ointment on your cut, okay? It'll probably tingle some." His steady fingers worked quickly, his touch considerate. "This might burn a little, but I'm going to need you to hold the gauze on there for me."

Shelby blew out a long stream of air but obeyed. Hopefully the deer had gotten up and continued into the forest. The image of an injured animal didn't sit well with her, especially when she felt fine.

"Good. Just like that," Joel coached. "Put pressure on it and hold it." He rocked back so he was sitting on his heels. "I should call for an ambulance."

"No." She grabbed his wrist as he reached for his

pocket and probably his cell phone. An ambulance meant that her brother, Caleb, would be called and he'd overreact. A lecture from him was best saved until morning. "I'm good. I could drive home if my car wasn't in the ditch."

"Then let me call for a tow truck."

So this Joel was persistent. And cute. He wasn't built and overly muscled like her brother, but he had a quiet strength about him. She narrowed her eyes. He actually looked familiar.

Shelby shook her head. "I go to church with the local mechanic. He has two small kids and I don't want to wake them up by calling him right now. I'll get in touch with him tomorrow."

Joel looked back up to the road. "If the cops see your car here they might give you a ticket."

"My brother's best friend is on rotation for the night shift this week. I'll send him a text to let him know about my car." Good thing Miles had recently made the transfer from the police force in the big city of Brookside to the smaller Goose Harbor department. It came in handy being buddies with one of the seven officers in town.

A slow smile lit Joel's face. "Everyone still knows everyone around here, don't they? It sounds like Goose Harbor hasn't changed a bit since I left."

Since he left? Shelby leaned closer. He smelled like cinnamon gum. *Joel.* She knew a Joel once… The image of a wiry teenager with midnight black hair, a closed-lipped smile and deep hazel eyes popped into her mind.

"Are you…?" It had to be. "Joel Palermo, right?" Caught up in the excitement of seeing an old friend, she grabbed both his hands. He couldn't have been more than sixteen when he left town some fourteen years ago.

He nodded. "And if I'm not mistaken, you're Caleb's little sister. Shelby Beck." He glanced at her left hand. "It's still Beck, isn't it?"

Her? Married? Right, he'd left before the fire. He didn't know about the scars marring her skin.

"Still just a Beck."

As teenagers, Miles, Caleb and Joel had been inseparable for the few years Joel lived with a foster family in Goose Harbor.

"It's so good to see you." She squeezed his hand.

He looked at their hands for a moment. "That's nice to hear. I didn't know how people would feel about me coming back."

She let go of his hand. What had come over her to latch on to him like that? Besides, they'd forgotten something important while they'd been catching up and taking care of her cut. "Wait. What about the deer?"

"Deer?"

"When you went to get your flashlight did you check the deer? How is it?" She jammed the deed papers into her purse, slung the bag over her shoulder and locked the car door.

He scratched his chin. "Um, I didn't take a look at the deer. I was more worried about you."

"Well, I'm fine."

"You're sure?"

"Listen, my head hurts like there's a small child jumping on my brain, but I'll survive. Nothing's broken. Believe me, I've survived much worse than a small accident." Shelby pressed past him and stumbled up the incline.

He grabbed her elbow to steady her. "Whoa, there. Let's walk easy. Maybe I should call Caleb for you. Does he still live in town?"

Shelby swallowed. When Caleb proposed to Paige Windom, Shelby made a promise to herself to move out of her brother's home and begin making a life of her own apart from Caleb. She needed to learn to be independent and stop letting Caleb take care of everything.

She spun around too quickly. "No. I don't want that."

Feeling woozy from the fast movement, she grabbed on to the first thing she could find to steady herself. That ended up being the fabric of Joel's coat near his chest.

Joel's arms came around her. "Listen, Shelby, I don't think—"

She spotted the deer. It rested in the gravel on the edge of the street. Shelby let go of Joel's coat and inched toward the animal. She fell to her knees beside her. No breath. No movement.

"Oh, you poor thing. I'm so sorry." Tears welled in her eyes. Shelby turned to Joel. He stood behind her, working his jaw back and forth. Hands shoved deep in his pockets.

"I killed her." She got up. Why had they talked so long? She should have climbed out of the car the second it went into the ditch in order to help the deer.

Joel shrugged. "It was just a deer. The important thing is you're okay."

She scowled at him. "We should have at least tried to save her. If we hadn't talked so long we might have been able to do something."

"Listen." Joel placed a hand on Shelby's shoulder guiding her away from the deer. "Even if we'd come up here right away and it was still breathing, it had three broken legs. Not to mention plenty of internal damage. We would only have been extending its suffering by trying to help."

Shelby pulled away from him. "Just because something was wrong with her—something she didn't deserve—doesn't mean she wasn't worth saving. Her life still meant something." Shelby fisted her hands to hide that she was shaking. Why did people only want something or believe it had worth if it was perfect—unblemished. The deer might not have been able to live in the wild again, but they could have taken it somewhere to rehabilitate it. Some zoo or nature preserve.

"She probably died on impact, Shelby. Accidents happen. Let's just leave it be."

"I didn't mean for it to die," she whispered.

Joel blew out a long stream of air. "Yeah, well, if I've learned anything in life, it's that a lot of things happen that we don't mean for, and a lot of hurt tends to happen along the way." He offered his hand and his voice grew softer. "Come on, let's get you home."

Joel was right about the deer, but Shelby hated that the animal had died. She slipped her hand into his and her gaze darted to his eyes.

It would be nice to have someone around who could get to know her without viewing her as the guarded baby sister, the way the entire town did.

Perhaps this time Joel wouldn't be only Caleb's friend.

Maybe he'd be her friend, too.

Joel gulped. Man alive, Shelby was pretty.

Lights from his pickup splashed across the pavement,

illuminating her. He marveled at her creamy skin. Red-brown hair cascaded just over her shoulders in waves, a couple of freckles dusted her nose and her eyes were as green as a summer meadow. The set of her regal little jaw told him she was trying her hardest not to cry about the deer.

If it was humanly possible, he'd kick himself. *Dummy.* He was so used to being around men at the firehouse; he needed to remember to phrase things more gently when talking to women. She probably thought he was some animal-hating brute, and for a reason he didn't want to think about, it bothered him that Shelby might peg him wrong on their first meeting as adults.

It felt more than nice, though, to have someone holding his hand like Shelby was. Tight—as if she trusted him already. No one had ever held on to him like that. Well, honestly, had he ever held someone's hand? Not counting the police officers who had pulled him away from his mother all those years ago. No.

He eyed the gash on her temple. "Are you dizzy at all?"

With her free hand, she hugged her stomach tightly. "I'm perfectly fine."

Joel glanced at her busted car. The rust bucket of a vehicle was a goner. He shrugged. A police report could wait until morning. "Come on. Let's grab your personal stuff from your car and get you into town."

"I have my purse. Everything else in there should be fine." She patted the small bag.

Good. At least she wasn't one of those women who toted around half of her belongings in a suitcase-sized bag.

He hesitated. "You're not afraid of dogs, are you?"

Shelby tipped back her head and laughed loudly.

Joel scratched his chin. "Does that mean no?"

"I own a dog-walking business. I got in the wreck on my way home from a dog-sitting gig. What do you think?"

"Well, that's good, because my guy, Dante, is in the cab. He's harmless, though. I promise. Where am I taking you?"

"I live on the main square, above Gran's Candy Shoppe."

"Unreal. That place still exists?" Joel rounded the truck and opened the passenger door for her.

Dante yelped and lurched forward, his tongue going into full action mode as he soundly licked Shelby's cheek. Most women would have shrieked, but Shelby scratched Dante's head and kissed him right on the muzzle.

Joel let out the breath he hadn't realized he'd been holding. Accepting Dante was as good as accepting him, if not better. Shelby Beck had just passed the most important test to winning Joel's trust.

The truck boasted a hole the size of a baseball on the floor. Shelby positioned her feet around the spot. Joel pulled onto the highway, the trailer carrying his motorcycle creaking along behind them. She stared at the radio dial. No sound. Maybe it was busted. Or he didn't like having it on. Either way, Shelby couldn't stand the silence.

She ran her fingers over the silky hairs of the dog's head and noticed his shape and colorings. He possessed the black-and-white blending of a border collie, but had patches of brown, as well. The dog gazed at her with crystal blue eyes. "This is an Australian cattle dog."

Joel looped his hand over the steering wheel and regarded her. "The lady knows her dogs."

Shelby shrugged. "Occupational hazard. He's beautiful. I love his markings. It's a boy, right?"

"Yeah. This is Dante. He's partially deaf so if you talk to him and he doesn't look at you, don't take offense. He's an old boy now, so he moves slow. But he's my best friend." Joel patted the dog on the rump and then left his hand resting there. "We found each other eight years ago and have been inseparable ever since."

"You found each other. That sounds intriguing."

The lights of the small downtown strip of Goose Harbor came in to view.

Joel kept his eyes on the road. "It wasn't a good time for me. I was…in between homes and found Dante wandering in an alley. He was so scrawny. His rib cage looked like blades jutting out of his body." He rubbed his hand over Dante's back. "I brought him to a local vet. The doctor recognized him right away. I guess they don't get a lot of Dante's breed in that town."

Recognized? "But you didn't have to give him back?"

"Turns out his owner died and neither of her two adult children wanted to take Dante, so instead of finding him a home they brought him into town and dumped him on the street."

"That's awful." Shelby gasped. "How can people be so cruel?"

"People—most people—just don't care beyond themselves."

The truck's tires thumped over the brick-paved block that made up the main square of the town.

"But how could someone not want Dante? He seems so sweet." Shelby scratched behind his ears and the dog sighed happily. "Who wouldn't want to open their home to him if they could?"

At the single stoplight in town, Joel bowed his head. Eyes closed, he took a deep breath. "They just didn't want him. No one wanted him. That's all there was to it," he whispered.

The light turned green and he pulled around the corner and parked in front of Gran's Candy Shoppe. A streetlight illuminated the interior of the truck's cab. Joel's smile was gone. His brow furrowed.

They just didn't want him. No one wanted him.

Joel had been in the foster system when he'd lived in Goose Harbor. An older couple from their church had taken him. After Joel disappeared, the couple had sold their home and moved to Florida.

She listened to Dante's even breaths for a minute. "Dogs are wonderful. I love them because they don't judge. They don't care if something's wrong with you. That's why I started working with them."

"Exactly. He's become everything to me." Joel scratched Dante's back.

Shelby leaned across Dante and placed her hand over Joel's. "I'm glad he found you."

"Me, too." The trace of something that wanted to be a smile pulled on his lips. He fished a pen and a folded receipt from one of the truck's cup holders. "Let me give you my number. Promise me that if you start feeling worse or your head starts hurting or you get dizzy you'll call me."

"Sure." She reached to take the piece of paper from him.

He didn't let go of it. "Anytime of the night. I'm serious."

She met his eyes. The intensity of his gaze made her catch her breath. "I promise," she whispered.

He let go of the paper. "Have a good night, Shelby."

"You, too." She grabbed her purse. "And take care of sweet Dante."

"Will do." Joel saluted her.

She laughed and made her way to the door on the side of the building that led up to her apartment, the whole time keenly aware that Joel hadn't pulled away until she was safely inside.

Joel straightened his shirt, took a deep breath and then stepped into the fire chief's office. Three chairs and a mammoth mahogany desk filled the small room, leaving him no choice but to stand in the small square of space in the open doorway.

Chief Wheeler hopped to his feet when he spotted Joel, a boisterous laugh making his red beard waggle as he offered his hand. "Great to see you again, Palermo. Are you settling into your new place all right?"

"I only just got in last night. I haven't even unpacked yet, sir."

"Well, take time to enjoy the town this week—chief's orders." He plunked into his chair.

"Will do." Joel sat in the seat across from Wheeler. "Is there anything else you need from me before I start?"

"Nothing I can think of, other than never call me sir again." He laughed.

"Chief?" A light tap sounded on the door. "Do you have a minute." Shelby Beck popped her head into the office. "Oh, I'm so sorry. You're busy. I can come back later."

"Hogwash. You know I always have time for you." The chief motioned for her to join them. "Shelby, I want you to meet our newest fireman, Joel Palermo. I believe he's about your age. If I recall correctly, he's also single."

A small grin played over Shelby's face. "We've met."

"I see." The chief winked at them.

She grabbed the last available seat in the room, which brought her knee to knee with Joel. Her smile was infectious.

He leaned forward to examine the cut on her temple. "How's your head?"

"Good." She moved her hair to cover the barely visible gash. "How's Dante?

Joel leaned back in his chair. "I'm sure he's happy to have a yard to sniff around in. Our last place didn't have one. He may be old, but he really likes being outside."

"You know," she began, "when you're on your days staying here at the firehouse, I could walk Dante for you and stop in to make sure he's okay."

Joel nudged her knee with his. "Look at you, Miss Businesswoman, adding me to your clientele when I've been in town less than twenty-four hours."

"No. I didn't mean—I'm offering as a friend." Shelby's cheeks flushed. "I don't want your money."

"I was kidding with you." He winked.

Chief Wheeler crossed his arms over his chest. "So, Shelby, I'm assuming you came in here to do more than just flirt with my handsome new fireman."

Shelby's cheeks blazed fire-engine red. "I'm not—"

Joel opened his mouth to defend her.

But the chief slapped the table and laughed. "I'm kidding, girl. Although, if you like him, I could order him to take you on a date."

Shelby looked down at the floor. "Like I said, I can come back another time if that's better."

Chief Wheeler adjusted his tie. "Relax, Shelby. What can I do for you?"

She knit her fingers together as she blew out a long breath. Then she tugged a bundle of papers from her purse. "My father left me this. I can rebuild. Finally. I'm going to meet with Ida today. When her husband was mayor, I remember him raising money for just that purpose. I want to see if that money is still available, but even if it is, I'm sure it won't be enough."

The chief sat a little straighter. "And you're asking if the fire department would help you raise more?"

"People love firefighters." She shrugged.

"Dashing men in uniform coming to the rescue. What's not to love, right, Joel?"

Unsure of the correct way to interact with his new boss, Joel only offered a smile.

The chief extended his hand to shake Shelby's. "Of course we'll help. In fact, Joel, since you're new around here, as your first order of business upon joining the department, I'm going to have you team with Shelby on planning a fund-raiser. You'll get to meet the whole town that way."

"Sure. Why not?" Helping host a fund-raiser was the perfect opportunity to get in good with the people of Goose Harbor, which was what he needed if this was going to be his forever home. He wanted them to forget the moody teenager who ran away. If he had tried, he couldn't have come up with a better way to enter the town again.

"I was thinking a pancake breakfast," Shelby piped up.

Joel leaned his elbows on his knees. "Food included. This gig is getting better by the minute. So, what are we fund-raising for?"

"To rebuild the church."

Her words hit his gut like a two-ton weight. *Rebuild the church?* There had been only one in town when he left. *But*—he swallowed hard. It felt like there was gravel in his throat—*it couldn't be.* "What church?"

Shelby touched his forearm. "The only church in town. You remember, don't you? Wait, you wouldn't because it was still standing when you lived here last time, wasn't it?"

Joel's heart beat so hard and fast he was afraid it showed through his shirt.

"What happened to it?" He had to ask since they thought he didn't know. Not looking curious would cast suspicion his way.

Shelby tugged on her sleeves and glanced at the ground.

Chief Wheeler cleared his throat. "It burned down, but I figured you knew that."

Of course Joel already knew.

Because fourteen years ago, he'd been the one who set it on fire.

Chapter Two

Joel's gaze followed Shelby as she left the chief's office.

Chief Wheeler rose from his desk, crossed the room and shut the door to his office. "Shelby is a very special young woman."

"Yes, I know." With the news about the church's destruction swirling through his mind, Joel couldn't quite make eye contact with the chief. What if someone discovered the role he played in the fire? Would he be able to justify his actions? He hadn't realized he'd destroyed the whole building. He'd only meant to ruin a wall or something of that magnitude. Just enough to send the message to God that he was not okay with what had been happening in his life.

"How well do you know Shelby?" The chief moved to the edge of his desk and scooted so he was sitting, which brought him very near to where Joel sat.

Relax. He commanded the muscles in his back and arms to ease. Focusing on Shelby helped, since she had nothing to do with the fire. "I knew her years ago. From when I lived here before. I was more friends with Caleb than with her, but she tagged along most of the time when we hung out…like an annoying little sister should."

He chuckled as a memory pushed its way into his mind, one of Shelby trying to chase after Caleb, Miles and Joel as they tried to sneak out of youth group to go waterskiing. When they wouldn't let her follow she went and tattled on them. The youth pastor made the boys clean the church's bathrooms every Saturday for the next month.

"A lot can happen in fourteen years, son." The tone in Chief Wheeler's voice changed on the last word. It became softer, kinder.

It sounded a bit like forgiveness. Or was Joel hearing things through the filter of misguided hope?

Joel finally met the man's eyes. "You're right. That's a lot of time. Life's moved on for all of us, and I'm just glad for the chance to be back, however long that is. Chief, I'm not sure how much you remember about how I was as a teen—"

"Enough." Wheeler grinned. The chief had been a regular fireman back then, and in a town where everyone knew everyone, Joel was aware that despite the buffer of fourteen years, some of his troubled past was still common knowledge in Goose Harbor.

"I'm not that kid anymore. I hope you know that."

"I wouldn't have hired you if I thought you were." The chief tugged a manila folder from the stack on his desk. "Speaking of which, I wanted to talk to you about the employee information form I asked you to fill out."

Joel gripped the armrest. *Please don't ask about Charlie.* Charlie Greave had saved Joel's life, let him live with his family while Joel pursued his training, and helped Joel land his first position in a firehouse.

Charlie had been the only lasting father figure he'd ever known, but then Charlie had left, too. Although, Charlie had fought his illness bravely, he'd lost. Joel didn't trust himself to talk about it.

Wheeler tugged a single piece of paper from the folder and handed it to Joel. "I think you forgot to list an emergency contact."

"No. It's all filled out." Joel refused to glance at the page. He didn't want to see the blank lines that he'd never be able to fill in. Name of spouse. Names and ages of children. He didn't know the first thing about how to be a good boyfriend, husband or father. All he had to offer a girl was a bunch of baggage, and if Joel knew anything, it was that he was man enough to save a woman that sort of disappointment.

Chief Wheeler stood and paced to the window in his office that overlooked the shopping district in town. "Why haven't you listed an emergency contact?"

"Because I don't have one." Why did his stomach feel as if he'd swallowed acid?

"No one?" The chief turned around to face him. "This isn't your first department, so I'm not going to pretend you don't know how dangerous our work can be. I do everything in my power to keep the people under my command safe. You understand that, don't you?"

Joel nodded.

"But I can't guarantee you won't get hurt." Wheeler crossed his arms over his barrel-sized chest. "Many a fireman has had to pay the ultimate price in order to save others."

"I'm aware of the dangers, sir." In fact, it was the

whole reason Joel had become a firefighter six years ago. The job made his life matter. Finally.

Wheeler's bushy orange eyebrows dove. "I thought I told you no more calling me sir."

"You did. I'm sorry. I'm just having a hard time understanding what you need from me."

Wheeler dropped into the chair Shelby had vacated. "You're telling me that if the worst should happen to you, there's no one in the world you would want me to contact? Not one single person?"

Joel shuffled his feet. "Is that a problem?"

"No relations? No friends who might wish to be told?"

Joel tucked his hands into his coat pockets. "My mom overdosed about a year after she got released from prison the last time around, and she's the only family member I knew of." He shouldn't have shared that. The chief didn't need to know about his personal struggles. He pinched the bridge of his nose. "I'm sorry. Why is this important to my paperwork?"

"I'm worried about you, Palermo. That's what. Not having an emergency contact could make you a reckless firefighter. I can't have you taking chances that'll harm my other men. An attachment outside of the fire keeps you sane."

The chief couldn't be letting him go. Not after Joel moved his whole life up here. How long would his status as an orphan be held against him? Until he died? No, the chief had done a bang-up job reminding him no one would mourn Joel when his time came.

Joel sat up straighter. "You have my paperwork from my last station. At my last post I was recognized for—"

The chief held up his hand to stop Joel's words. "I've

read about your accolades and awards. You're a member of a standby hotshot team. I'm not minimizing that at all. What I am saying, however, is that the rest of this department has strong ties to spouses, children, parents, longtime friends or extended family. When they're in a burning building they can keep their cool and make decisions because in the back of their minds they're reminded they have someone who needs them at home. It adds a layer of…weight to their work that keeps them from putting themselves and others in unnecessarily dangerous positions. You don't have that."

"Well, I'm not sure what you want me to do exactly. There's still no one I can add to the line for emergency contacts. Not one person in the world would miss me if I was gone." He tried to swallow, but his throat felt so tight. Dante was the only creature on earth that'd even miss him.

Chief Wheeler gripped Joel's shoulder. "Want to know how you can fix this for me? Find something worth coming home to."

Shelby ran her sleeve across her forehead. It might only have been the start of summer, but the temperature was already rising. And riding across town on two half-filled bike tires didn't help, either. She'd yet to hear back from the mechanic about her car, but hopefully the old Volkswagen could be saved, because she wouldn't be able to bike to all her dog-walking locations. While she was happy her small business had taken off in the past month, she didn't love driving all over the county in order to make enough to pay rent. If only she could find a way to merge her love of animals with something that would keep her from having to commute from house to house.

Ida Ashby lived in a small cottage just to the right of the West Oaks Inn bed-and-breakfast. The cottage could have popped right off the page of a fairy tale.

She licked her lips, grabbed hold of the copper knocker and knocked.

"Well, now, come on in with you," Ida's soft, sweet voice called through one of the open windows.

Shelby eased open the door. "Hi, Ida."

"Hi there, sweet thing. What brings you down my way?" Though she had been alone in her house, Ida wore a dress. Her hair was pulled back and her Mary Jane shoes shimmered below her crossed ankles.

"I hate to sound rude, but I came to ask you about some money." Shelby fidgeted with her bag.

Ida set down her mug of tea and peered over her glasses. "You look a mite old to be selling cookies door to door, but if you are, I'll take two boxes."

Shelby laughed. She needed to make it down to see Ida more often. The woman was a riot.

"Nothing like that. I promise. Although, if you want cookies, I'll bring some along next time I stop in." Shelby winked at her. "Actually, I was coming to ask about Mayor Ashby. He—"

"My Henry was a good man."

"The best."

Ida nodded her head solemnly. "The love of my life. He still is, you know. The heart doesn't forget great love."

Shelby puffed out a breath. Great love? Let's see, a father who had run out on her mother when she was diagnosed with cancer, and no male prospects in her own life because of the scars on her legs, arms and back. It didn't look like any *great love* would be coming Shelby's way any time soon. She'd have to live vicariously through her brother and Paige if she wanted to experience love.

Shelby cleared her throat. "I came to talk to you about something a little more important—"

Ida's eyes went wide. "Oh, sweetheart, there is nothing in the world more important than love. Absolutely nothing. Even the good Lord says so in the Bible. He says there is hope, faith and love—but the greatest of those is love."

"I suppose that's true."

"There's no supposing. It just is. You make sure to look for chances to have love in your life. It comes in all forms and at the most quiet moments. Sometimes it tiptoes right on into our lives when we're being too loud to notice it."

"I'll try to remember that."

Ida smiled and picked up her mug. "Was there something else you needed, dear?"

Shelby licked her lips and leaned forward. "I was young, so I might not remember correctly, but didn't Mayor Ashby start a fund meant to rebuild the church?"

"Oh, was he ever heartbroken when he found out they couldn't go ahead with plans for the church." Ida laid her hands over her heart. "It was his dearest wish to see our little chapel standing again. I've always been rather unhappy about the fact that Henry didn't get to see it happen in his lifetime. But he couldn't convince the church board to keep the land. They were so bent on washing their hands of the building and moving on so the congregation could divide. It was a very sad time for us."

"So there was an account set up for the church?"

"Not *was*, dear, there *is* one. I advised him to divert the money to another worthwhile purpose, but he just wouldn't see the reason in that. My Henry was such a dreamer, you see. He held out hope that someday an opportunity to rebuild would resurface."

"I think we might be able to." Shelby unfolded the deed to the land the church used to occupy. She showed it to Ida. "My dad passed away recently."

"Oh, I'm so sorry."

"It's okay. We weren't close. We hadn't spoken in years."

"How tragic." Ida closed her eyes for a moment.

"The important thing is we can rebuild the church, Ida. My dad left me the land in his will. I just need to know if there are enough funds, and if I can access them."

Ida clasped her hands together and rocked back and forth as she stared at the piece of paper. "My Henry would be so pleased. I should have known he'd be right all along. That was his fondest wish. You do know that, don't you? He'd say this was the happiest day of his life—besides our wedding day, of course."

"Of course." Shelby nodded along.

"Paperwork." Ida shuffled over to a metal filing cabinet that was four drawers high. "Let me see here." She pulled out a file a few minutes later. "Right here. Yes. My Henry was so brilliant. You see." Plunking the paperwork on the table, she jutted her fingers to indicate the first few lines. "He set the account up as a nonprofit whose sole purpose was to rebuild the church. That way, some of the greasy-fingered board members couldn't get a hold of the money and do something silly with it. You know the type—the ones who want to spend thousands of dollars on new street signs so we can look fancy for the tourists."

Ida explained that since her name was on the account, she would need to sign all the bills with regard to rebuilding the church. "And I'll be just delighted to sign whatever you bring me, because I trust you, my dear. I do. You'll do right by this community and finally give us our shiny white pearl back in town."

Shelby sure hoped she was up to the task.

Her phone rang as she waved goodbye to Ida. The screen told her it was her brother. "Hey, Caleb."

"I'm worried about you." In true Caleb fashion he cut right to his point.

"What's new? You're always worried about something." Shelby grabbed her bike off the ground.

"You're going to go ahead with this plan to rebuild the church, aren't you?"

"Of course. I told you that after the reading of Dad's will."

"I don't know if that's wise." He paused. "I mean, do you really want to bring up that bad memory again?"

Yes. That was where she had been burned. Why was he talking softer? As if it was a secret he didn't want others to find out. He could say it. It wasn't as if anyone could hear them.

"Don't you see? That's why I *have to* rebuild it." She wouldn't say the words out loud because Caleb would tell her what she felt was irrational, but ever since the fire, a part of her had felt trapped inside the ashes of the old church. Not long after the fire, she'd come up with the idea of rebuilding the church because it seemed like the only way to finally let go.

Caleb sighed. "Just tell me if you need something or if you need to talk or…you know. Anything." The tone of his voice made it sound like he meant deep, serious talking, not simply an update about the church.

"Talk?"

"If you go through with it—rebuilding the church— it has the potential to drag up some really hard times for you. I'm here. That's all I'm saying."

"Thanks, but I'll be fine. Hey, I've got to go. I can't ride my bike and talk on the cell at the same time."

"I just love you, Shelb."

"I know you do."

How could she make him see? Rebuilding the church wouldn't open old wounds.

No. It would finally heal her.

Joel strolled past the blazing-red fire engine, letting his fingers trail over the cool metal.

He caught a reflection of himself in a tinted wall of glass and froze. How would people react if he told them the truth about the church like he'd originally planned to? Of course, he couldn't do that now. Not after hearing that the church had burned all the way to the ground. When he'd set it ablaze all those years ago, he figured he'd char a section, at most, before the fire engine arrived. Just enough to get his point across to God, since He hadn't listened to Joel's cries. Joel hadn't stuck around long enough to find out the total damage.

It had seemed like a great idea to his sixteen-year-old self.

Without a doubt, if people knew what he had done,

they would treat him differently again—like they always did. Not just differently. They'd probably run him out of town. Certainly, Chief Wheeler would fire him. And Joel wouldn't blame him. Who would keep a fireman with a history of arson on the payroll? Now no one could ever find out. His happiness in Goose Harbor depended on it.

When he first saw the listing for a position with the Goose Harbor Fire Department, he'd prayed about it. After a week of praying, he had known he was supposed to apply. Now he wasn't so sure. Why had God brought him back to the scene of his greatest failure? Last time Joel had left town, he'd been so angry at God for dashing his hopes once again, but he'd made peace since then. God wasn't the enemy, just selfish humans like his mom and the people who had cast aside Dante. Really, God was the only one who'd ever accepted him as is.

Probably the only one who ever would.

Maybe he shouldn't have come back to Goose Harbor, after all. It had been a fool's dream to think he could return without the past dogging his heels everywhere he went. But he was here now and needed to make the best of his new life. For starters, if he knew one thing, it was that staying on the chief's good side was rule number one in fire department code. The chief wanted him to work with Shelby on a fund-raiser, so he'd do it.

There was a bright side: working with Shelby. Joel wouldn't mind getting to know her better or spending hours beside the pretty woman. Not one bit. She'd been cute when he last lived in town. Just a scrawny thing made up more of knees and elbows than anything else. She'd had braces back then, and hadn't tamed the curl in her hair like she had now. The years had been good to her. Maybe spending time with her could knock out the other thing the chief wanted him to find—something worth coming home to.

Cool down, Joel.

Focus. The chief was wrong to encourage him to get attached. People failed him. Always. He was here to finally feel like he belonged somewhere. Getting involved with a woman wouldn't help that. It would only provide a reason to leave when things fell apart.

Like they always did.

His life could count for the work he did, the lives he helped save, whether from fires or as an EMT coaxing a teen to get in the ambulance instead of taking more pills and ending it all. Each act, each day, was penance for him. Perhaps at some point, he'd think he was good enough for God and for a woman. But not now. Not yet.

Who was he kidding? Probably not ever.

The knot that had been forming in his stomach since he first decided to return to Goose Harbor unwound just a little. After having been a firefighter for the past six years, being in a station set him at ease.

The engine, the axes, the gear—these things he knew and understood. The outside world, well, he couldn't say the same when he walked out of the building. He didn't know the first thing about relationships, putting down roots and creating a future—all the things he hoped for and dreamed about. Once he walked out the front doors again, the knot in his stomach would tighten right back up.

The wolves of his past howled in his mind. *Not wanted. Not good enough. Not worth it.*

Four days after his sixth birthday, Joel became a

ward of the State of Michigan. Even at that age, he'd known his mother couldn't take care of him.

Unwelcome images projected onto his mind's eye, stop-action pictures reminiscent of an old scratchy movie. A bone-thin woman with flaxen hair sat cross-legged at a table with a razor and white powder. Men filtered into the apartment one after another. Uncapped syringes on the counter, and Mom with a green bottle in her hand laughing. Angry yelling and people coming after her. Mom passed out on the kitchen floor.

Joel batted his hand in the air to shoo away the thoughts. That was a long time ago. A different life. He steeled himself against the image of the dark-haired little boy crouching in the corner of his memory. At thirty years old, he wanted nothing to do with that child anymore. The past needed to stay there. Locked tightly away, key tossed in a murky river.

Now he had a fresh chance to prove his worth. And that would include never telling anyone about the fire and everything else in his life he was ashamed about. No matter what.

"Joel?" Someone walked up behind him.

He turned. "Caleb? Is that you?"

Caleb stepped forward and, before Joel realized it was happening, his old friend was giving him a tight, quick man hug. Joel thumped him on the back twice.

Stepping back, Caleb smiled. His old friend hadn't changed much. He was still bigger than Joel and looked as if he lifted weights every day. Caleb had always had the outdoorsman look.

"It's great to see you. I heard through the rumor mill at the old Cherry Top Café that you were back in town, so I came here to see if it was true."

Joel shoved his hands deep into the pockets of his jeans. "I'm glad you still live here."

Caleb shook his head slowly. "You're back, right? For good? Not just visiting?"

"Back indefinitely. I start here at the department on Wednesday."

"I hear you and Shelby are working on a fund-raiser."

Only in Goose Harbor. "Word travels fast here. I found out about that myself only an hour ago."

Caleb held up his phone. "I just hung up with her." His old friend stepped closer. "It sounds like she's pretty excited to get to know you again. I wanted to say…I'm worried. Shelby's special."

"That's what everyone keeps saying." Joel braced his shoulder against a doorjamb.

"Everyone?" Caleb's voice instantly became a growl. "Who's everyone?"

No matter how pretty Shelby was, a man would be foolish to tangle with Caleb. Even when they were teens, Caleb had fought to protect his family like a lion over the last piece of meat. Joel was smart enough not to step into that battle.

"Forget I said anything."

Caleb glanced past Joel to the lounge room in the firehouse where a few of the other men played on the Wii. "Who have you been talking to about Shelby?"

"Cool down." Joel grabbed Caleb's arm and pulled him out of earshot of the other firefighters. "Just Chief Wheeler and only because she showed up here."

Caleb paced a few feet away. "When you spend time with her, please don't lead her on, okay? Keep it professional."

"Sounds like you're telling me to stay away from

your little sister." Joel didn't know why he was poking an agitated bear. He didn't have any designs on Shelby. How could he when he hardly knew her? But he challenged Caleb all the same. A lifetime stuck in foster homes following new, and sometimes ridiculous, rules made Joel bristle when someone told him he wasn't allowed to do something as an adult.

"I am." Caleb crossed his arms over his chest. Same old Caleb.

Joel titled his head. "Tell me, you do realize she's not twelve anymore? I don't know her, but I'm sure Shelby's old enough to take care of herself."

"She's not—"

"Like I said." Joel raised his hands in the universal sign of *let's-drop-this-already.* "I don't know her. Your warning is a bit premature, buddy. I just got into town last night and, between you and me, romance isn't even a blip on my radar."

"That's exactly when it finds you."

"Well, no worries for me and Shelby. Okay?"

His old friend lowered his voice. "Maybe it's not the time or place to ask you this, but where did you go?"

"When?" Joel stalled for time, but he had known the conversation would come to this. *What happened that day?* If Caleb questioned him, Joel would have to think quickly and place himself far away from the church.

"You said you'd meet me at the bend in the river so we could fish that day and…you just didn't show. Do you know how heartbroken the Lloyds were when you never came back? They thought of you like a son."

Like a son? Right. That's why the Lloyds told him they were going to turn him back over to the state so they could move to Florida on their retirement money.

Joel laughed once, drily. "Is that what the Lloyds told everyone? That I ran away from them?"

Caleb frowned. "They asked everyone to help find you and formed search parties. They were so upset they moved away a few months later. I think they had to get away from the memories and the hurt from not knowing what happened to you."

Joel's hand formed a fist in his pocket.

Relax. Mr. and Mrs. Lloyd had been good people. They'd opened their home to him for three years, and he'd been a handful the whole time. He shouldn't have expected more. Never should have allowed his mind to entertain the thought that they might make him a permanent part of their family.

But he couldn't let Caleb believe he'd run off for no good reason. "It sounds like they didn't tell anyone they'd decided to turn me back over to Child Protective Services. Nice of them to leave that bit out."

Yes, Mrs. Lloyd's arthritis had progressed to the point where she couldn't hold a toothbrush, but hadn't Joel been there to help them? He might have been a hardheaded sixteen-year-old, but he'd cared enough about the Lloyds to have helped them however they needed. When the doctor had told them that living somewhere warmer might help Mrs. Lloyd, they'd immediately put a move in motion. Sure, they'd petitioned the state for permission to take Joel, but, even then, he'd known they would never have been granted authorization. Not with his mother still alive. Even if she had been in jail.

And when they weren't, they still chose to move instead of keep Joel. Still decided to hand him right back to the state.

Caleb's brow furrowed. "They were going to give you back?"

Joel nodded.

"Man. I'm sorry. I never knew."

"Yeah." Joel crossed his arms tightly over his chest. "Within ten years, I'd lived in twelve different places. I was so sick of being sent wherever my case manager deemed best. For once, I wanted to be in control of my future—if that makes sense. I couldn't go back into the foster system. Not after enjoying three years in Goose Harbor. I couldn't live like that any longer."

"So they were right—you took off?"

He shrugged. "I ran away, if that's what you're asking. You've got to understand, I was so mad at God and everyone that I just…I needed to do life on my own for a while. Live by my own terms."

"And how'd that go for you?"

He hadn't forgotten how tenacious Caleb could be when it came to getting to the bottom of an issue. Like a mosquito in search of exposed flesh.

Joel ran his finger over the grooves in the cinder-block wall. "It went badly." He let his hand drop to his side. "Let's see, four years in an out of homeless shelters in Indiana. I had to take the GED since I didn't graduate high school here, and sending for my transcripts would have tipped off my case manager. Anyway, I always wanted to come back. I've thought about Goose Harbor a lot over the years."

Caleb placed his hand on Joel's shoulder. "You were missed. I always wondered what happened to you. I never stopped praying for you." He squeezed Joel's shoulder.

Joel straightened his shirt and stepped away from Caleb. "Looks like those prayers might have worked."

"I have to head out to finish end-of-the-year non-sense at school, but we should catch up more. You have to meet Paige, my fiancée. She's a teacher, too. Know what? You have to come to our wedding. The invitations have already gone out, but I'll get you the information."

They made plans to grill steaks later in the week on one of the days Joel wasn't scheduled to work a twelve-hour shift, and then Caleb headed out.

When he'd left years ago, Caleb had been going steady with Sarah West, had been since grade school. Caleb and Sarah had always talked about getting married, but it sounded like that hadn't happened.

Which made sense. What kid actually got his child-hood dream? Joel sure hadn't. Which was fine. Dreams changed. He no longer begged God for the family he'd never have. No, his requests were simpler now. The conversation with the chief nagged at him. Perhaps Wheeler was right. It would be nice to have someone in the world besides Dante to miss him if something happened.

One person. Was that too much to ask?

Chapter Three

Pink-and-orange sunlight pushed the purple of night out of the sky as Shelby dipped her toes into the brisk lake water. Minnows danced in a group near the shore and a large dragonfly buzzed over the surface of the calm water. The sand under the water was hard and compact beneath her feet. On warm summer mornings, she planned to swim out to the end of the pier and back for exercise, but today the water was still too chilly. Lake Michigan always took too long to warm up. For now, she'd wade. Just wade.

Her father had taught her to swim on this same beach, and before the divorce, her family had spent every summer weekend here with a picnic and volleyball. This beach was the only kind memory of Dad she allowed herself to hang on to. In grade school, she'd been a part of the swim team at the local Y, but after the fire, she quit.

Oh, Caleb and Mom told her no one would treat her differently. They said she should wear her scars with her head held high because those marks on her skin meant she had survived a great tragedy. They said people wouldn't even notice them.

Caleb and Mom had been wrong.

People had been polite to her face—if openly staring at the burned patches on her arms, back and legs could be considered polite. But Shelby had heard them whispering. She'd seen people trying to avert their eyes from her ugliness. Some of her friends at school had even been afraid to touch her, as if the scars were contagious.

That's when her wardrobe had changed to all jeans and long sleeves no matter what. The only time she shed those concealing clothes was for her morning swim in summer and when she was by herself in her apartment. And when she was alone around animals. Animals didn't judge.

She ran her fingers on the two tougher, bright pink patches of skin on her arms. The marks might as well have been labels stuck to her that read: damaged goods. Like a dented can of string beans in the reduced food section of the store.

Because of the scars, she'd never know the joy of marriage that Caleb and his fiancée, Paige, were about to experience. Nor would she get to hold her firstborn child—or any child of hers in her arms. The day the church caught fire, those dreams had ended. They'd been crushed right under the same beam that had fallen from the ceiling and trapped her.

Who would want her like this? No man.

Knee-high in the water now, she scanned the beach. It was too early for anyone to be up and near the shore. Even the joggers hadn't ventured out yet. She usually saw them on her way back to her car. Granted, today she'd taken longer to get to the beach since she'd had to ride her bike.

Today's swim would need to be cut short so she could put her clothes back on before anyone saw her in her swimsuit. She probably shouldn't have come anyway. It was too early in the summer yet for the lake water to be a swimmable temperature.

She escaped the cold water and toweled off her legs before slipping on her baggy jeans and hooded sweat-shirt. Glancing at her watch, she remembered she was supposed to meet Joel this morning at Fair Tradewinds Coffee. The small coffee shop was off the beaten path so most of the tourists who swarmed the town during the summer didn't know about it. She loved the place.

She needed to get a move on.

She and Joel had a fund-raiser to plan and a church to build.

Hands in his pockets, Joel crossed the grassy town square and followed the wide walking path that led to a strip of businesses lining the shore. A few of the shops he passed had already turned their signs to Open, but other than the crew from a single cargo boat unload-ing packages at the far end of the wharf, the town was quiet. Most tourists stayed tucked safety in their rented homes and bed-and-breakfast rooms until at least ten in the morning.

Joel breathed in the early-morning air. The lake's surface was calm, but Joel, an expert at appearing com-posed no matter what was going on inside, knew just how deceiving looks could be.

He'd agreed to meet Shelby at the mom-and-pop cof-fee place near the harbor this morning since he was free—his first stretch of workdays wouldn't start until tomorrow. Might as well get the fund-raising planning over with so he could wash his hands of any church business as fast as possible.

Fair Tradewinds Coffee was easy to find because of the rusted old boat lift attached to the part of the shop that hung over the water. The building was a reclaimed relic dating back to the town's founding as a port for shipping lumber to Chicago. The large sign hanging from the old boat lift read: Try the Screaming Joe. It's Just the Lift You Need!

He pushed through the front door. The coffee shop took nautical decorations to the extreme. An old boat mast served as a middle support column, burlap coffee bean sacks hung on the walls and a large white sail was suspended like a billowing cloud from the ceiling. The baristas were dressed like sailors.

Despite how quiet and sleepy the town had seemed, almost every seat in the coffee shop was taken except for the couches near a potbelly stove. And he guessed they were available only because of a sign that read the section was reserved.

"Hey." Shelby waved from a small table that butted up to one of the couches.

Joel nodded to her but stopped at the counter to order a drink before grabbing a seat. Shelby wore a sweatshirt big enough to belong to her brother. For a minute, Joel wondered if she'd met him in her pajamas, but no. She wore jeans and her hair was wet, so she'd clearly taken a shower and chosen to wear the tent-like shirt.

"What'd you order?" She pulled a notepad out of her small bag and grinned at him.

"The Screaming Joe."

Her mouth fell open and eyes went wide. "You didn't."

"I did." He smiled.

"Have you ever tried it?"

"I'm about to. Why, should I be afraid?"

"They put hot sauce in the coffee," she whispered.

"I'm sure it's fine." He winked at her and then took a big swig. Huge mistake. A burning rushed down his throat and filled his chest. He coughed, eyes watering.

Shelby covered a wide smile with one hand and shoved a wad of napkins at him with the other. "Not so bad, huh?"

"Wow." He wheezed and shoved the cup of offending coffee to the center of the table. "I think that's about half hot sauce and half coffee."

"You're new in town, so I'd say it was eighty percent hot sauce."

"I'm afraid to try anything else here." He laughed.

"Everything else is safe. The Screaming Joe's on the menu because of Robert." She pointed at a man who looked like a seventy-year-old in the body of a thirty-year-old. "He owns the place and says he's in such good shape because he drinks a Screaming Joe every morning."

"He can have mine." Joel caught himself grinning like a child again. Shelby was so easy to joke with. It was refreshing. It helped that they already knew each other, because the get-to-know-each-other part of friendships was the part Joel disliked the most. "So, what are your thoughts for this fund-raiser?"

"Okay." Shelby flipped over the first page of her notepad to reveal a sheet of notes. "I called the local scout leader last night and he volunteered his group to be servers at our pancake breakfast. So, between them and the youth group kids that Paige and Caleb work with, we're set there. Maggie West said she'd round up some local women to help cook that morning. We need to set a date, decide on a location and secure the ingredients as donations. What else? Did you have some ideas?"

"I...um." To be honest, he hadn't thought about actual details for the fund-raiser at all since the chief told him he'd be assigned to help. "The chief said we can hold it at the firehouse."

"Oh, good." She bit her lip while she jotted that down. "I figured, I mean..." She stared at something over his shoulder.

Joel glanced behind him. A group of five men finished their orders at the front counter and then claimed the couch area right next to them. When he turned back to Shelby her hands were braced on either side of her face, her elbows on the table. Her eyes bored into a napkin as if it was the most important thing in the world.

"Do you know them?" Joel leaned closer to her and kept his voice low.

"They all go to the church I attend—the singles group." She didn't look up.

One of the men behind them must have spotted Joel and Shelby because he said to his friends, "Did you see her?"

"That's Shelby, isn't it?" They clearly thought they were talking low enough not to be overheard. "How long do you think she'll give the new guy?"

"Only gave me three dates."

"Me, too."

"It's always just three dates. Then she decides she's

too good for whoever she's with. Poor loser. I wonder what date he's on now."

"Forget her. She's pretty, but she's not worth the time and trouble."

"Right. I'm happy I found Brenda."

"When's the wedding?"

Joel couldn't make sense of the conversation. The chief and Caleb both called Shelby special, but that didn't jibe with what the men from her church were saying. With how they were acting, he wasn't surprised that Shelby had dumped them all after three dates. In fact, he was more surprised they'd made it to the third if they thought it was okay to talk about a woman like that while she was within earshot. Still, he wondered what had happened. Had Caleb flexed his muscles and convinced Shelby she shouldn't be with them? Or had he issued warnings like he'd done already to Joel?

Shelby dashed a tear from her cheek and shifted in her chair as if she were about to make a run for it. Why had he let her sit and endure that conversation?

Joel snaked his hand across the table and grabbed hers. "Let's get out of here."

As they left the shop, she clutched his hand tightly, the way she had the first day after the car accident.

And he didn't mind one bit.

Shelby swallowed hard. "I'm sorry you had to hear that. I can explain." But could she? No. Not without saying she'd broken off every relationship once she started to like the guy—once she had realized she would eventually have to tell him about her scars.

What must Joel think of her after hearing those men? There went any hopes of a friendship with him.

Even so, Shelby dug her fingers into the back of Joel's hand like it was a lifeline. She gulped warm air as he led her down the boardwalk that followed the beach to the old lighthouse, which marked the edge of Goose Harbor. Shelby had held hands with a small number of men in her life—her father, Caleb and a couple of guys she'd dated. Not one of them had hands like Joel Palermo—rough and calloused, but with fingers long enough to be a concert pianist's.

He looked out at the lake. "Think we can make it all the way to the lighthouse?"

"Joel—"

"It's already pretty warm, but if you're game, I am."

"Don't pretend you didn't hear those guys." She dropped his hand and faced him. "I know you did."

He shrugged. "You don't owe me an explanation."

She fiddled with the strap on her bag and looked at her shoes. "But I don't want you to think that I…"

"I don't think that."

Her eyes met his. "You don't?"

He stepped closer. They were already standing close so now he was only a breath or two away. "Believe me, I know better than to let other people form opinions for me."

"Okay." She stepped back, putting a couple of feet of space between them. "But if you don't want to spend time with me after that, I understand." Why had she said that? Again and again she shoved people away before they had the chance to reject her.

"Shelby, I don't know if you've noticed, but no one's forcing me to spend time with you." He laughed and held up a hand. "Okay, technically the chief is forcing me to spend time with you, but I'm glad because without him I'd have to think of an excuse to do the same."

"You don't ever need an excuse." She wondered if he heard her words; they were so soft.

"Good to know. Come on." He motioned for her to keep walking with him down the boardwalk. "Dante would love this. I've never taken him to a beach before."

"Once you do, you'll have to bring him here every day." Shelby caught his gaze out of the corner of her eye and then glanced away. Something about spending time with this man put her at ease and gave her a chance to be herself more so than with anyone else recently.

"Unfortunately, with my work schedule, he'll be lucky if I take him here twice a week."

Right. Firefighters worked long hours that often included overnights. "Like I said before, Joel, I could walk him for you. On the days when you're working or busy. I wouldn't mind at all. He's such a pretty dog."

"Handsome," Joel corrected her.

"Right. Handsome." She winked at him. "I'm sorry if I talk a lot. Caleb says I talk too much. He says I can't handle silence." Why had she just said that?

"That's fine. You can talk as much as you'd like around me. I've had enough silence to last a lifetime." He cleared his throat. "So, how'd you get involved with all this church stuff?" He'd been looking at her before, but now he gazed out at the lake.

Don't tell him about her involvement with the fire—not yet.

"After the fire, my dad purchased the land the church sat on."

"The community just sold it—easy like that?"

"I don't know if you remember, but the congregation

had a big rift right before the fire. More than half the members had already left to start a church in a movie theater in Shadowbend." She pointed to indicate the town north of them. "Those who were left didn't donate enough to pay the bills to keep the church doors open. To most people, it made more sense to sell the land and move on at the time."

"But not to you?"

She shrugged. "I miss having a church in town."

"Then why didn't your dad rebuild?"

"Oh, he bought the property because he had grand plans of segmenting the land and selling it off for development. He saw dollar signs. But the town board stopped him with zoning laws, tax issues and as much red tape as they could find." *Thankfully.* "Mayor Ashby always wanted the church rebuilt."

Joel stopped and faced her, rocking back on his feet. "I find it hard to believe your dad didn't look into all that before making that kind of an investment."

"Really? I mean, we're talking about the same guy who met a woman on the internet and walked out on his family a month later to be with her. He's never really been a think-it-through kind of guy."

"But to hold on to it like that? For so long—with no return on his investment?" Joel scratched his head.

"Spite can make people do a lot of crazy things." She pressed past Joel and started walking up the boardwalk again. The side closest to the beach was sandy, but on the other side tall clumps of dune grass grew. Shelby lifted her hand so the top of the blades tickled her palm. "Honestly, I don't really know his reasons…he and I didn't talk after he left."

"Never?"

"Never."

"I'm sorry."

"I am, too. But he passed away recently and there's nothing I can do about that. He left me the land, so I figured I can finally do right and rebuild."

"Whoever you hire for the construction, just make sure they don't rip you off."

"Do you know anything about rebuilding?"

"A little. I worked construction for two years before becoming a fireman. Some contractors have ways of up-charging and taking advantage of people who don't know what's needed and not needed. Not all contractors are like that, but be careful."

"Maybe I'll have you look at the plans when I get them." She nudged him good-naturedly with her elbow.

"I'd rather not help with the church." Joel stopped, did a half turn and then raked his fingers through his hair. "That sounded bad. I'm fine with the fund-raiser, but when it comes to the actual church building—not that I have anything against the church, I'm a Christian, but…man, it's hot out here already. Maybe we shouldn't walk all the way to the lighthouse."

"It's warmer than usual." Shelby stopped herself right before she pushed up her sleeve.

"Do you want me to carry your sweatshirt?" Joel held out his hand.

"No. I'm fine," she lied. "I'm not even hot."

"You're sweating." He tapped his forehead.

She used her sleeve to wipe the sweat off her brow. "I'm fine."

But she wasn't—not because of the heat, but because already in their first time hanging out together she'd been reminded why she couldn't ever be more than friends with Joel, even if she wanted to be. Her scars had already caused tension.

She'd have to keep better control of her emotions, because as nice as it was to forget about her problems and talk with Joel, it wasn't worth the pain she would feel if she started to care about him and he eventually rejected her.

Chapter Four

He shouldn't have come here. Didn't he know better? But he pressed down the kickstand to his motorcycle and climbed off the bike anyway.

Crossing his arms, Joel surveyed the land where the Community Church of Goose Harbor once sat. Visible from everywhere in town, the white spire topped with a cross had been the tallest point in Goose Harbor. Until he burned it down.

If he could go back in time… If he could have a redo… If he could…

Joel shook his head. Entertaining what-ifs never helped anyone.

He raked his hand through his hair and then stepped over the small metal fence that closed in the area. Not worried about the sign that said Private Property Keep Out.

Weeds and knee-high grass covered the area. Some litter collected where the wind had blown it against the fence. Nature had taken over, but a trained eye could see the outline of the old church foundation, where the basement probably still was. Other than that, this piece of land could have been any other abandoned lot.

Joel dragged his fingers over the top of the long grass as he walked. When he had lived in Goose Harbor as a teenager, this was where he'd become friends with Miles and Caleb. They hadn't had any classes in school together—what with him being held back a year at one point—but youth group had served as an equalizer. For the first time ever, Joel had known friendship and belonging. He'd wanted to stay.

Right here.

He'd learned about God and had opened up to the possibility that his heavenly Father might love him, even if his earthly father had not.

Joel sighed. Where he stood was about the place the old youth pastor's office would have been—where Joel had been given his first Bible and had prayed with the pastor to become a Christian. When he closed his eyes, he could picture Pastor Brent in his dress pants and gym shoes, always ready to talk, and constantly reminding them they were all loved.

And it was all gone because of him.

Joel closed his eyes, bowed his head and prayed out loud. "I'm so sorry. I see now what one rash act of anger can do. I never meant to destroy this building. In the last fourteen years, You and I have come to a good spot—not without a lot of me digging in my heels and fighting You—but we're here and I'm thankful. When I've strayed, You've come after me time and time again. We may be on right standing these days, but I know I never asked for Your forgiveness over what I did to this church. Please forgive me, Lord. Let me move on in this town."

Asking for forgiveness didn't feel like enough. Joel had ruined another person's property and he owed that person an apology. He should tell someone. He really should. Didn't the Bible say Christians were to confess their sins to each other? Pastor Brent had moved away from Goose Harbor, but perhaps Joel could track him down. The man had always been easy to talk to.

Then again, maybe it was enough to ask God's forgiveness. Ultimately, the church was His. And if that was all Joel had to do, then there wasn't a need to face any consequences that might come with fessing up to a long-ago crime. Especially since telling the truth would ruin any chance he had of putting down roots in this town. Not to mention it would probably get him fired. What was that phrase? Silence is golden. Yes, he'd stick with silence.

The sound of a car on the street behind him made Joel open his eyes and turn around. The flashing emergency lights of a police car reflected off the metal of his motorcycle. The police car parked nearby and an officer with large mirrored sunglasses climbed out.

Joel's mouth went dry and his stomach corkscrewed. For a moment, he contemplated taking off at a run, but he wasn't some kid in trouble. If the officer wanted something, Joel would have to deal with it like a man. But his palms started sweating all the same. The policeman couldn't know he was linked to the fire. Could he? Whatever it was, Joel knew all cops were bad cops. All the ones he'd known over the years sure confirmed that.

"Can I speak with you, sir?" the officer called out as he crossed the street. Why did every cop possess the same purposeful stride? Maybe they took a class in the police academy called How to Walk Intimidatingly. If so, the instructor deserved a raise for a job well done.

Joel cleared his throat. He hated that his childhood fear of the police could still make him nervous. "What seems to be the problem, Officer?"

"Let's see. For starters, you're trespassing on private property." The officer was getting closer.

Joel stepped over the low fence again. *Keep calm.* "I believe it's only considered trespassing if you're not welcome on the land. It so happens I'm friends with the property owner. We could call her if you'd like to verify that. She won't mind that I'm here."

The officer tugged off his sunglasses and smiled. "Well, I'll be—Caleb and Shelby said you were back in town. I was planning to look you up at the firehouse later today." His old friend, Miles, held out his hand.

Joel shook it. "Glad we bumped into each other before then." He should have recognized Miles right away. Just like Caleb, Miles hadn't changed much in appearance since high school. "So, there's no trouble with me being on this property, then?"

"Not now. Fact is, I heard you're working with Shelby to rebuild." Miles hooked his fingers on his duty belt and scanned the vacant property. The gold star pinned on his chest glinted in the morning sun. "It'll be nice to have a church here again. We've been meeting in a movie theater in Shadowbend for more than ten years. I'd really like to go someplace where my shoes don't end up stuck to the floor and my clothes don't smell like popcorn by the end of service."

"Actually, I'm not rebuilding it. I'm just helping with the fund-raiser." Joel rubbed the back of his neck.

Miles wagged his head and whistled low. "You have

no idea how persuasive Shelby can be, then. She'll have you out here balancing on scaffolding by the end of the week, if it's up to her."

"Not likely," Joel mumbled.

Miles raised his eyebrows. "Just wait." He eased his stance a bit. "What brings you back to Goose Harbor, anyway?"

Had Caleb told Miles the truth about why Joel had left town? For some reason, he hoped not. Old friend or not, he wouldn't be able to trust Miles. Not now that he was a cop.

Joel worked his jaw back and forth. "Are you asking me as a cop or as a friend?"

"I'm both. I don't think I can separate the two."

He rolled his shoulders, forcing the muscles under his coat to relax. "Weren't we always dodging the police after curfew? I never would have figured you'd cross over to the dark side and become an officer."

Miles barked out a laugh. "If I've crossed over, then you have, too. Police and fire are both first responders. We're basically the same."

"They're not even close to being the same. People actually like firefighters." Joel smirked.

"Oh. You slay me. Really, Joel." Miles put his hand on his chest and pretended to be offended. Then he straightened back up. "In all seriousness, I'd forgotten how much you hated the police. We're not all bad."

"Yeah, well." Joel unclipped his helmet from his motorcycle. "When your only interactions with them are as a kid being put in the back of the squad car because your parent don't want you, I guess it's hard to form a decent opinion of them."

"If it helps, the police are like any other profession.

There are good ones and bad ones. But by and large, we'd lay down our lives to help someone we didn't even know, just like when you rush into a fire."

"Speaking of which, I need to get to work. It's my first day. Probably not the best impression if I show up late."

"I won't keep you, then. Tell the chief I said hey and that he still owes the department pizza from when we won the chili cook-off."

"Will do." Joel nodded and pulled out the key for his bike.

"One last thing." Miles positioned his sunglasses on his face. "You have only a month to update your license and registration. Make sure you do that because, friend or not, I'll have to write you a ticket if you don't."

Right. All cops were bad cops. Even Miles.

Joel would have to be careful not to restart their friendship because, like Miles had said, he couldn't separate who he was from his job. Joel didn't need to be friends with someone who someday could arrest him for an unsolved arson in town.

"Everyone will think I look silly." Shelby stared at her reflection in the bridal shop's floor-to-ceiling mirrors, which showed every angle of her body. The celery-green dress shimmered when she moved. The shimmer wasn't the problem. The issue was that the dress was ankle-length with an accompanying mother-of-the-bride-like blazer.

Paige, her future sister-in-law, came up behind Shelby and cupped her shoulders. "You look beautiful, like you always do."

"But you're having an outdoor wedding. In summer.

People will think I'm crazy wearing clothes that cover every inch of my skin." Or maybe they wouldn't since she always covered up. She liked to imagine her day-to-day wardrobe choices didn't stick out so much, but up in front of everyone in this dress, she might as well wear a flashing sign. Shelby shrugged off Paige's hands and turned around. Away from the wall of mirrors.

"Shelby…" Paige took a deep breath.

"I know you want to say something."

"It'll sound mean."

"Just say it."

"I don't know why you feel the need to cover up everything." Paige played with the hair tie she wore around her wrist. "People know. It's not like they don't."

Shelby shook her head. "Actually, a lot of people in town don't know. I mean, they know I was in the fire, but they've never seen the scars. They have no clue what I look like, and I'd rather it stay that way. And as for the couple of people who have seen, the last time I showed my scars I was thirteen, so I'm kind of hoping they've forgotten how bad I look. Or maybe they'll think I've healed."

Paige bit her lip. "Well, you have some options."

"Like?"

"For starters, people won't think you're crazy for wearing the long sleeves. They'll think I'm the loony one. The bride gets the blame for what the bridesmaids wear. It's part of my job. They'll all think I was so afraid of you outshining me that I had to cover you up."

"Nice try, but Maggie isn't wearing this dress, and she's your maid of honor."

"She said she would if you wanted her to. You know Maggie wouldn't mind."

Shelby glanced back in the mirror. She really looked ridiculous. The outfit was designed for someone a good forty years older than she was. Although, she had no one to blame but herself, since she'd insisted on an outfit that covered her arms and legs. "I'm not making Maggie wear head-to-toe fabric in the middle of summer."

"There is another option." Paige tilted her head.

"I'm listening."

"You could wear what Maggie's wearing." Paige pointed at the dress hanging on the sidewall, a sweet little frock that scooped at the neck and floated out at the knees. Maggie would look so cute, and Shelby would have loved—for once in her adult life—to wear something like that. Instead, she'd look ridiculous all alone.

She blinked back tears. "You know I can't wear something like that. Didn't you hear me? I just said I don't want people to see."

"You could," Paige's voice grew soft.

Shelby whipped around. "My scars would show." She dashed the hot tears off her cheeks.

Paige spoke gently, "Caleb's said it to you time and time again, and I'll say it, too. You're the only one letting that hold you back from life. We don't even see them. We just see beautiful, sweet and kindhearted Shelby, and that's all anyone would see if you'd let them."

Easy for Caleb and Paige to say. For starters, Paige was a gorgeous blonde. In Shelby's opinion, her brother's fiancée could secure a job tomorrow as a runway model if she decided not to be a teacher anymore. But more than that, Paige hadn't lived with the stares and people stepping away from her once they saw her skin. There was a good reason Shelby hadn't let anyone see the marks in almost fourteen years.

Paige hadn't had to break up with two great guys before the relationship became too close. Each time, Shelby had cut it off before she had to tell them. What was the use? There wasn't a reason to date any longer—not once she'd realized no man would want her when they could have a wife whose skin glowed in a cute sundress.

"You guys don't get it," Shelby mumbled, shuffling over to the changing room. She closed the door and tried to keep the rest of her tears from falling. She fanned her face for a minute and then peeled out of the coat and dress, sucking in deep breaths to try to calm down. The wedding was only one day. For one day, she'd have to stand in front of a large crowd with everyone wondering why she was dressed like a grandma. She could do it for Caleb and Paige. She had to.

As she hung the dress on the hanger, she caught sight of the large scar on her back. It was the size of a dessert plate, located almost in the center of her back, but a little to the left. It marked the exact spot where the ceiling beam had pinned her to the ground. Another scar, as long as an unsharpened pencil but three fingers thick, ran from wrist to elbow on her right arm. The left arm had faired a bit better with only two small patches— one on her forearm and one small spot on her biceps. She looked away before assessing the backs of her legs.

Shelby finished dressing quickly and then left the changing room, matronly dress in hand.

Paige waited for her on a plush couch near the front of the small store. "What did you decide?"

"You don't really need me to stand up in your wedding." Shelby dangled the dress behind her by hooking the hanger on her fingers and resting the back of her hand on her shoulder.

"Of course I do. You're my new sister. Besides, I already paid the clerk for it." Paige stood and held the front door open for Shelby.

Another cloudless blue sky met them outside. It was going to be a hotter than normal summer.

Shelby walked beside Paige to where Paige's car was parked. "But doesn't Caleb still only have Miles standing up in the wedding? It would look better if just Maggie and Miles walked down together. I'll be this awkward third wheel in front of everyone."

"You're not getting out of this, missy. We'll just have to double our efforts to convince Caleb to ask another guy to stand up." Paige's car chirped. "Hey, what about this Joel guy?"

Shelby thought of him and smiled. "Joel would definitely look great in a suit, and he and Caleb were best friends when they were teens."

"And you wouldn't mind walking down the aisle with him—not one bit, would you?" Paige's hand shot out and squeezed Shelby's free one. "He's cute, am I right? I can tell by how you said his name. And a fireman. That's perfect. Everyone loves a fireman. I can't wait to meet him."

"I'm actually going to the firehouse now to see him." It was only a short walk from the bridal shop, and then she'd double back to her apartment and pick up her bicycle.

"Are you now?" Paige's voice rose and she waggled her eyebrows.

"Yeah, I need to pick up his house key."

"Shelby, I don't know if you should—"

"Wow. My overprotective brother has already rubbed off on you. Relax, okay? Joel's giving me a key so I can check on his dog when he's on shift at the firehouse."

"So, do tell." Paige grinned. "You two seem to have clicked right away. Are you thinking romance? I'll definitely have to meet this man and see if he's good enough for my Shelby."

"Paaaige." Shelby drew out her name. "Don't embarrass me. And it's not like that. At all. He's just a friend. Less than that. He was Caleb's friend and I was just the little sister."

"Ah, but you're all grown up and wonderful now. He'd be a fool not to see that."

"We're both better off just staying friends." Shelby hugged the dress to her stomach.

"Shelby, you've got to start letting people love you."

"I do."

"More than just family."

"A lot of people in town love me."

Paige rolled her eyes. "Okay, I mean a man—romantically."

"That's not for me."

Paige leaned against the side of her car. "Why not?"

"Let's not get on that topic again." Shelby turned to leave. She wouldn't go through this conversational loop again. Paige was a sweetheart, but she could be like a bloodhound stuck on a scent trail when she wanted to prove a point. Yet another reason she and Caleb were perfect for each other.

"Because of the burns? Shelby…" Paige caught her arm and stopped her from walking away. "Someday you'll have to let someone in. Why not now? A man—the right man—won't care one bit about your scars."

"That's not true. Even *I* think they're ugly. How can I expect someone else not to?" She held up her hand. "I know you've seen pictures of my mother. She was so beautiful, probably the prettiest woman I've ever seen in real life. But what did that get her? Even being that beautiful, my dad still left her. What chance do I have, if she couldn't convince a man to be faithful to her when she didn't have anything wrong with her?"

"That's not a fair comparison, Shelby, I—"

She stepped back. "I need to get going."

"Me, too." Paige checked her watch. "I'm supposed to meet with the florist in half an hour." She pointed at Shelby. "This conversation isn't over. There are still some things I want to say and some things I think you're wrong about."

Shelby waved goodbye and started down the sidewalk.

The conversation was over. Forever.

Chapter Five

Joel twisted the faucet and warm water rushed into his cupped hands. He splashed his face. No matter how many fires he responded to, he'd never get used to reeking of smoke afterward. He had been in the house for only a few minutes, and in full gear, but the smell had leeched into his hair and seeped into every pore. Prior experience had taught him he could scrub with industrial soap, but he would always smell smoke and ashes days later.

Chief Wheeler opened the cabinet near Joel's head. He grabbed a mug with an advertisement for an insurance company plastered on the side. "Everything good at the Amsted residence?"

Joel grabbed the kitchen dish towel and scrubbed it over his wet face and hair. He'd replace it with a fresh one. As the newbie, he'd been assigned laundry duty on his first shift. "If by good you mean their kitchen is charred and their house is no longer structurally sound, then sure."

"You know what I mean." Wheeler groaned when he found the coffeepot empty. "These guys act like they think their moms live here." Yanking open a large drawer, he dug out a packet of coffee and dumped it on top of the used filter and grounds already in the machine. Joel grimaced. That explained why the coffee this morning tasted like tar.

Wheeler jabbed the orange "on" button and then turned around and leaned against the counter so he faced Joel. "Tell me about the fire."

Why wasn't the chief seeking out the on-duty lieutenant and asking him?

Joel tossed the dirty towel into the hamper near the doorway. "Mrs. Amsted and the baby were both in the house. It was the usual—she put something in the oven and forgot about it. The baby's a newborn, so Mrs. Amsted is understandably tired and she'd fallen asleep while the baby was napping. She said they'd yanked the batteries out of their smoke detectors a few weeks ago when she burned dinner. Good thing their neighbor saw the smoke."

"But everyone's okay?" He pinned Joel with an intense stare and crossed his arms over his wide chest.

Joel shifted his weight between his feet. He felt like a bug under a microscope. Why the inquisition? "We took them to the hospital to get checked over. They'll be fine. Some of the windows were open, so the smoke hadn't gathered in their rooms as much as we often see."

"Know what I like about fires?" Wheeler spun back to the coffee machine and filled up his cup.

There was nothing to like about fires. Okay, controlled fires were a different story, but they weren't talking about that kind. "They give us a job?"

"Good point, but no." He turned back around and took a swig from his steaming mug. "I like that every fire is a chance to start over. A fire offers a unique opportunity to have a new beginning."

Joel thought back to the empty lot he'd stood in just this morning. New beginning? The church lot had sat untouched for almost fourteen years. Not much of a new start. "I doubt the Amsteds feel the same way right now."

The chief waved his hand in a dismissive manner. "Mrs. Amsted has been bugging her husband for years about remodeling that kitchen. Now she'll get a brand-new one."

"A new kitchen?" Joel fought the edge in his voice. During his years working in Indy and then doing a tour with a hotshot forest fire team, he'd seen too much destruction caused by fires. Too many lives lost and ruined. He couldn't be flippant about that suffering, and it bothered him that his chief would talk in such a way. "No disrespect meant, sir, but I feel like you're making light of their pain."

"Not at all." The chief's voice grew softer, kinder. "I know the Amsteds well—just as I've known most everything that's happened and everyone in this town for the past twenty years." He paused for a moment, made eye contact, then continued. "They're thankful and praising God their family is safe today. Tomorrow, they'll rebuild and be stronger, closer, because of the fire. Coming out the other side of a tragedy has a way of teaching you what's important in this life."

"Sounds like you're saying a fire is a blessing, and I can't agree with you there." Joel couldn't look at the chief. He couldn't make eye contact or he would say something that could get him in trouble. Still, he had to add something so Wheeler would knock off the talk about fire being wonderful. "At all."

"You're a firefighter."

"Right." On the other hand, perhaps it was best to state a logical case. "So I know how damaging a fire can be. Maybe I've pulled one too many…" Stop. Talking about the people he'd failed in the line of duty only brought their images back to his mind. "My job—our job—is to minimize destruction and to rescue people so they don't get hurt. Not to celebrate when fires happen."

"Have you ever seen a field the year after a grass fire?"

Joel shrugged.

"It's healthier. The soil has more nutrients and more animals can thrive off the same piece of land than before."

"Yeah, and some animals died in the original fire." Joel grabbed the hamper. He might as well get on the laundry. At the very least, it would give him a reason to bow out of the conversation.

"True. I'm not minimizing the fact that fire causes pain and sometimes has lifelong ramifications. I guess my point, for you to ponder specifically, is that sometimes the rebuilding after a fire—well, you see, that's when the real rescue comes."

"If you say so." Joel stood in the doorway with the laundry basket.

"Just promise me you'll think about that."

"Will do." Joel nodded and headed down the hall, but halted because Shelby Beck waited a couple of feet away. When she smiled, it made him forget about fires and smelling like smoke. He just wanted to stand there, stare at her and forget about everything.

She tilted her head. "He's right, you know."

"Who?" What was she talking about?

"Chief Wheeler." She jutted her thumb to indicate the kitchen Joel had just left. So she'd overheard the conversation. "Rebuilding after a fire can be a really good thing. It can be healing. Like it'll be with the church."

He scrubbed his free hand across his jaw. How come the church had to come up every time he talked to Shelby? "The church doesn't count. No one was hurt by the church fire." Not that anyone was hurt today, either, but they could have been. A child could have been injured, which hadn't been the case with the church.

Shelby's mouth opened. Then closed. Then opened again. She looked down at the ground and her voice came out very small. "A...a lot of people were hurt by that fire." She looked back up at him and her eyes brimmed with unshed tears. "Lives were ruined."

Ruined? A queasy feeling washed over his gut. Now it was his turn to stall for time. Joel glanced at the dirty laundry and studied a washcloth with a spaghetti stain shaped like Australia. "What do you mean?"

"I mean...that was the community's church home." She studied the floor again. "That's all."

He stared at her face. Something about the fire was very personal to Shelby, and for that he was sorry. He wished he could tell her it was his fault. Maybe it would help if she could blame someone. But that wasn't going to happen.

That was close. She'd almost blurted out about being in the church. About how personal the rebuild project was to her. Someday maybe she'd share it with him. Joel seemed like the type of person who would be compassionate, but—no, she didn't want his pity. And that was all it would be. He'd feel bad for the marred girl and then pull away.

Change the topic.

He was watching her closely. With his messy head of black hair, he was an attractive man. It gave him a bad-boy quality that didn't quite fit the usual firefighter persona. Maybe it was because she knew he rode a motorcycle, and the first time she saw him he'd worn a leather jacket.

Joel shifted the laundry basket and his biceps strained against the sleeves of his blue T-shirt, which was adorned with the fire station's number.

Shelby fidgeted with the hanger for her dress. Why hadn't she left it in Paige's car like they'd planned? "Let's talk about something else."

"Sure." He sighed.

She frowned. A spot of soot dirtied his temple and there were lines around his eyes. "Are you okay?"

"Of course." A lazy grin crept across Joel's face. "I'm great now."

"It's just, you look tired maybe." She leaned against the wall. He was still staring.

"No. I'm fine. We just came back from a fire. That's all."

"Oh. I can come by some other time." Shelby moved to head back down the hall.

Joel followed her, laundry basket snug under his arm. "Stay. Now's a perfect time. Come on." He motioned for her to follow him. They wove down the hallway until they arrived at the laundry room, which boasted two sets of washers and dryers. Joel tossed open one of the washer's lids and dumped the contents of the hamper into the tub.

"Aren't you going to separate the whites from the colors?" Shelby's fingers itched to fish all the dirty towels out of the washing machine and do the laundry correctly.

"I like to live dangerously."

"I'm being serious."

Joel laughed, dumped soap into the washing machine and then hit the start button. "For a bunch of dish towels? No thanks."

"They'll fade quicker that way."

"I don't think one guy here will mind using a faded towel."

"But—" She reached around him to stop the washing machine. If she'd learned one thing from living with Caleb, it was that some men needed help in these areas of life.

Joel caught her wrist and her sleeve pulled up a bit. "Shelby—"

She jerked away from his touch. Hard. The force made him bump backward against the washer. Shelby spun around and pulled at the sleeves of her shirt. She balled up her hands so they were completely covered by fabric. Had he felt her scar? He must have. His fingers had been wrapped right around it. What if he'd seen? Would he treat her differently?

Blinking back tears, she debated leaving until Joel placed his hand on her shoulder and slowly turned her around.

"Hey, I'm not sure...did I hurt you?"

"No. I'm fine. Great." She focused on the ceiling in an effort to keep the moisture inside her eyes.

"Are you sure?" He kept his hand on her shoulder. "Because you're acting like I hurt you."

"You didn't." Shelby finally met his gaze.

He was in EMT mode again, his eyes roaming back and forth over her face, reading her. "Feelings count, too."

"My feelings are fine." Breathe. He either hadn't noticed her skin or he was choosing to ignore it. Either way, she was happy not to talk about it.

"One thing you pick up when you've lived with a bunch of different families is how to read people. Unfortunately, I've had a lot of practice." He dipped his head to look into her eyes. "And you keep using the word *fine*, but you're not acting like you are."

She shrugged. How had stopping by the station for a key turned into a stilted conversation about the church and him almost discovering her secret? "I just wanted to separate the wash."

"I know." He nodded. "But it didn't need to be separated. It's okay not to do things perfectly sometimes. Live a little, Shelby. It's fun." It looked as if he was pressing his lips together to keep a smile under wraps.

"Are you laughing at me?" She narrowed her eyes, but fought a smile, too. All the tension from a moment ago drained from the room. Joel seemed to possess the ability to know when she needed to be encouraged, when she needed a challenge and when she needed to be teased into a lighter mood.

"Maybe." He winked.

"Not allowed." She grinned. "I already have an older brother, and it's his job in life to make fun of me."

"One, I don't want to be like a brother to you. And, two, I wasn't making fun—just trying to help you take things less seriously."

Less seriously? "What are you saying?"

"I'm saying I've only been back around you for a couple of days, but I already have you pegged."

"Oh, really? Do expound, Mr. Psychologist."

"Have a seat." He patted the top of the dryer and she obliged. Joel laced his fingers together and cracked his knuckles. "Let's see if that Psychology 101 course paid off." He winked at her again. "You've been sheltered your whole life. Probably not by choice, but there it is. So you do things a certain way. Thanks to Caleb, you probably believe there's good reason to be cautious and not take risks. Even silly ones that don't bother anyone and aren't necessarily wrong."

"There are lots of reasons not to take risks."

He tapped his watch. "The doctor's still in session."

"Do go on." She shook her head good-naturedly and laid the dress she'd been clutching next to her on the dryer.

"You're right. I'll be the first one to tell you not to take dangerous risks. But something like, say, mixing rags that a bunch of men used to sop up messes—it's probably okay not to waste energy doing that the correct way. Am I making sense?"

"So, basically, you think I don't know how to have fun."

"Well, I didn't say that."

"What's the diagnosis then, Doc? How does a girl cure herself from an overwhelming desire to make sure the laundry is separated even if it doesn't matter?"

He tapped his chin. "Take a few safe risks."

"Such as?" She hooked her ankles together and swung her legs.

"Come for a ride on my motorcycle."

Her mouth went dry. "Right now?"

"No. I can't. I'm on duty." He leaned against the washing machine and crossed his arms. "But later this week when I'm off duty."

"And that'll cure me?"

"It'll be a start." He smiled. "How about if that goes well, we'll come up with a new risk after that?"

"Don't get greedy. Only one short motorcycle ride. That's all I'm agreeing to." She hopped down from the dryer. "Now, didn't I come here to get a key from you?" She held out her hand.

"And an address." Joel fished the spare house key out of his pocket, told her where he lived and gave her instructions for Dante. He dangled the key on a chain over her outstretched palm. "How about we go on our motorcycle ride after we meet on Saturday to talk through donations for the fund-raiser?"

On Saturday the whole town would see them, because almost everyone spent time at the local farmer's market that took place in the square. And that made her look forward to it even more. For once, she wasn't going to care what everyone else thought about her.

"Sure, why not?"

"That's my girl." He grinned and finally dropped the key into her hand.

She closed her fingers around the warm metal and left the station with the words *my girl* playing over and over in her mind.

Chapter Six

Joel slowed his motorcycle as he turned down the street
leading to the grassy town square. An open patch of
concrete near the gazebo worked perfectly as a make-
shift parking spot. He left his bike with the helmet resting on top.

In typical early-summer fashion, a slight breeze
drifted from the direction of Lake Michigan. It might
still have been morning, but the temperature was already higher than normal. If Joel hadn't ridden his motorcycle, he would have worn shorts, but the motorcycle
meant jeans. He'd have to change before he took Dante
for his walk.

The people of Goose Harbor loved their weekly
farmer's market. Residents, as well as tourists, mingled between booths and visited near the park benches
and small rose garden on the edge of the grassy square,
which served as the heart of the town. This was the spot
where babysitters were found, rumors were spread and
teenagers began hanging out for the weekend.

When Joel last lived in town, the mayor and board
members had passed an ordinance prohibiting chain and

big box stores within city limits. Because of this, the closest grocery store was in Shadowbend. But townspeople usually only left Goose Harbor when they were low on packaged staples such as flour and sugar. Eggs, milk, bread, baked goods and produce all could be picked up fresh weekly here.

"If it isn't my sweet little Joel."

Mrs. Clarkson latched on to his forearm. Her hands were rough with age. She'd been considered an old lady when he had been a teen. By now, she must have been ancient. In her cat-eye glasses and home-sewn shirt, she was hard to miss. Her shirt looked like it had been made from pieced-together socks.

Once a week, after classes let out at the high school, Mrs. Clarkson used to pay Joel ten dollars to vacuum her house. Even though the chore had taken only thirty minutes to complete, he'd always been at her house for at least two hours afterward visiting. Did she still make those peanut butter cookies with the chocolate kiss in the center? His stomach rumbled at the memory. He probably should have eaten before he'd left his house.

"Look at you." He placed his hand over hers and gave it a light squeeze. "Still just as pretty and stylish as I remembered."

"Stylish, my eye." She swatted at his chest. "You were always a joker, but in the end such a good boy. I'm glad to see you finally decided to return home to us."

Such a good boy. Hardly. If she knew the truth, even kindhearted Mrs. Clarkson wouldn't be wasting her breath to welcome him back. She had played the piano for the church choir and had told him once that using the instrument was her only way to serve God. Had Joel, with the fire, taken that from her?

Shelby waved at them from the gazebo and then picked her way through the crowd. A large messenger-type bag bounced on her hip with each step.

"Mrs. Clarkson, is this ruffian bothering you?" She smirked at Joel.

Glad for the change of subject, he placed his hand over his heart and turned to Mrs. Clarkson. "Do you hear how she talks about me?"

The woman patted Joel's arm. "Shelby, dear, you need to be nice to our prodigal son. We don't need him getting any ideas and taking off on us again."

Her words were like a punch to his gut. He swallowed hard. *Taking off on us again.* Would they ever see him as someone other than that sixteen-year-old kid? If only she knew how much he'd wanted Goose Harbor to be home. That he'd never wanted to leave. Couldn't they see he really hadn't had a choice?

Why hadn't some kind, sweet old woman taken him into her home when he had been a teen? Joel would have loved someone like Mrs. Clarkson, crazy outfits and all, if she had let him. But she wouldn't have let him. Because no one wanted him in their family.

Probably still didn't.

But he'd show them. After all, he was an EMT and a firefighter. He rescued people for a living. How could they not like him? In fact, that would be his way to win them over. If they saw him as Joel-the-firefighter, then they'd want him. Joel just needed to work hard to blot from their minds the memory of Joel-the-troubled-youth, Joel-the-runaway and Joel-the-orphan. Because he didn't want their pity. He'd never wanted it. Only their acceptance.

At first, he'd been unsure about the idea of helping

with the church fund-raiser because of the past, but
when he had walked Dante the previous night, he'd realized that working with Shelby was his best hope for
moving forward in Goose Harbor. Not only would he
be the new firefighter in town, but people would think
well of him for giving so much time toward rebuilding
the lost church. This project was the perfect opportunity to win respect again.

"Oh, don't you worry." Shelby grinned at Mrs. Clarkson and then winked at Joel. "He's not allowed to go
anywhere because I need him."

"Do you, now?" Joel stepped closer, bringing an almost instant pretty flush to Shelby's cheeks. He'd never
noticed the way her eyes turned different colors de-
pending on the light. Her features were so small, they
gave her a vulnerability that made him want to tuck her
under his arm and take care of her.

Mrs. Clarkson chuckled. "It sure looks like Shelby's
not the only one who knows how to needle a body. I've
seen this all before and I think I'll take these old bones
to get a seat and watch how this plays out."

Had Mrs. Clarkson observed the way he'd looked at
Shelby? Evidently.

Joel held out his hand to the elderly woman. "Do you
want me to help you?"

"I may be old, but I'm still tough as Monday morning. Don't you worry about me." She waved and headed
into the crowd.

Shelby looked at her hands and tugged on her sleeves
so they reached the palms of her hands. "When I said I
needed you, I meant for the fund-raiser, of course. That
was…I hope you don't…you know."

Why did she always wear long sleeves? The ther-

mometer must be reading in the upper eighties already
and it was only morning.

"Of course." He offered his arm in a playful ges-
ture. "Shall we?"

Like in a black-and-white movie, Shelby took Joel's
offered arm and cupped her hand over his biceps. He
smiled at her and she couldn't help but shake her head
good-naturedly at him. Other than Caleb, no other man
walked around with her on his arm—especially not in
public. But perhaps that explained everything. Joel was
being brotherly. That was all.

Whatever the reason, he possessed a talent for making her feel at ease. Even when her brain was overana-
lyzing things, which she needed to stop doing around
him because she kept making them share awkward moments—such as the one at the firehouse and just a minute ago.

Joel raised his eyebrows. "So, what's the plan today?"

"I made these informational flyers." She tugged a
sheet of paper from the bag slung over her shoulder.
Unable to sleep much last night, she woke up early and
made handouts to give to the businesses. They described
the fund-raiser and her hope of rebuilding the church.
"I figured we could go door-to-door and use them to
try to get donations for the silent auction."

He took a flyer from her and scanned it. "Silent auction? But I thought we were doing a pancake breakfast."

"We are. We're doing both." The tilt of his head told
her she needed to explain. "What I mean is I thought it
would help bring in more donations if we held a silent
auction at the pancake breakfast."

Joel handed back the flyer. "You do realize we're doing this fund-raiser a week from today, right?"

"Yes." She tucked the flyer into her bag. Maybe the silent auction was a dumb idea. "Why?"

"Well, it sounds like we still have a lot of kinks to work out before we can make a go of this. Do we even have items for the auction? I've helped with these kinds of events before when I worked in Indy. Auctions take a lot of work to run. I'm not trying to discourage you, so don't hear me that way. Whatever you decide we need to do, I'm going to support it. My only caution is we don't want to commit to something we can't see through to the end. That's all I'm saying."

"There will be no kinks. Just work." She motioned so he would follow her toward the businesses that lined the town square. "Are you afraid of a little work, Mr. Palermo?"

"Not at all. Lead the way."

Two hours later they stopped by the firehouse to drop off their donations. The chief had offered Shelby the use of a drawer in his office for storing their supplies.

All the walking had caused her to work up a sweat so the air-conditioning inside the station was a welcome change. She'd been fighting the desire to roll up her sleeves all day. She knocked on the chief's door.

"Come on in," Wheeler's voice boomed. Not because he tried. He just had one of those voices that always sounded as if he were shouting.

As they entered, he stood up and straightened some files on his desk. One had Joel's name printed on the label. What sort of information did it hold? Probably just certificates for classes and training logs—those kinds of things. But what if the paperwork held deeper information? Like something that would help her better understand his past and get him to open up to her? She chided herself for being so curious.

"Looks like you two have been busy." Wheeler opened up the blinds in his office. Sunlight flooded the room and showed trails of dust on every surface.

Shelby opened her bag to unload some of their bounty. "We spent the morning telling all the business owners about the fund-raiser and got some donations for a silent auction."

Wheeler leaned over his desk to get a better look. "An auction. What a great idea."

"Joel didn't think so." Shelby jutted her thumb at him.

"Hey." Joel held up his hands. "I didn't say that. I just don't want you biting off more than you can chew and stressing out."

She'd noticed he usually went quiet around the chief, as if he was nervous because it was his boss. Maybe he didn't remember how kind Wheeler had been when they were kids. Of course, she thought of Wheeler differently because they shared a special bond. He was the firefighter who had lifted the beam off Shelby and carried her out of the blaze all those years ago. They'd stayed close after that. She couldn't begin to count the number of times he'd visited her in the hospital as she'd recovered. He'd sent flowers to her after every single skin graft surgery, as well.

If she were being honest, Wheeler had become somewhat of a replacement father to her. She prayed he'd become a trusted mentor in Joel's life, too, because even a thirty-year-old man needed someone to look up to.

Wheeler made three *tsk* sounds and shook his head.

"I guess you don't know Shelby well enough yet, but this lady is stronger than concrete. Nothing will stress her out."

Perhaps she'd hidden her bad days too well if Wheeler thought of her like that. Even right now, stress bubbled just under the surface like water in an over-heated teakettle. The mechanic had let her know her car was totaled, and she didn't have enough money in her savings account to replace it. In fact, she didn't have enough money in her savings to meet basic needs like paying rent and buying groceries for more than the next three months.

She already had called all her clients who didn't live in Goose Harbor and told them she couldn't walk their dogs or watch their homes while they were gone. She was losing so much money by not having a car.

After this fund-raiser, she would need to start applying to the stores in town to find a summer job so she could save up enough money to at least buy a junker and restart her dog-walking business later on. Or figure out a way to work with dogs without having to constantly travel for work. That would be ideal.

Wheeler reached for the paperwork in Shelby's hand. "Let's see how you did."

"Everyone was very generous. Founder's Creamery gave us a certificate for one free cone a week for an entire year. Maggie gave us an overnight stay at the West Oaks Inn. Clancy at the hardware store is having a sign made that reserves a spot in front of his store for the rest of the year—which is huge because it's so hard to find parking in the summer and he's right on the square. Free parking passes to the beach. Cooking classes at The Butcher's Block Café. A bunch of other stuff like that."

"Sounds like you guys did great."

Shelby stepped to the side to make room for Joel. She wanted him to feel like he was part of the conversation. "It was all Joel's doing. Turns out he's a smooth talker."

Wheeler dropped back into his chair. "I could have told you that. I interviewed him!"

Joel shuffled his feet. "I'm standing right here."

"Smile, son." The chief rested his elbows on his desk. "Most people never get to hear others say kind things about them. Whenever you're blessed enough to be in the room when someone's complimenting you, soak it up and be thankful. Too many people's lives are filled with hearing nothing but the negatives."

Joel nodded once while he scuffed his hand back and forth over his jaw. "Shelby, are you ready to get going?"

"Joel's taking me for a motorcycle ride." Shelby offered the information to Wheeler as they headed out the room.

"Be safe." The chief's voice followed them out into the hall.

"I always am."

Joel grabbed the handle to close the door as they left.

Shelby followed him to the section of the station where the men stayed while on duty. The living area smelled like a mixture of mustard and roast beef. Joel pulled his leather jacket out of his locker.

He pressed the worn leather into her hands. "It'll probably make you too warm. I didn't realize you'd wear long sleeves today. But I'd feel better if you wore my jacket, too. It's a safety thing."

She slipped it on. The fabric inside was soft from

wear. Shelby pressed the collar to her nose when Joel wasn't paying attention. It smelled like the cinnamon gum he always chewed.

They walked the two blocks back to the town square. Vendors at the farmer's market were packing up their booths, but many people still milled around visiting. Joel pointed to his bike parked near the white gazebo.

Shelby didn't know a lot about motorcycles, but she thought the kind he owned was a racing bike. Or something like that. It was small, with green detailing on the sides, and looked as if it could travel really fast.

All morning she'd pushed the thought of her motorcycle ride with Joel to the back of her mind. First, because she hadn't been sure he'd remember or ask her to follow through on her promise from the other day. Second, because she'd wanted to focus her attention on the fund-raiser, which was proving difficult whenever she was around Joel.

Honestly, she felt a little like her thirteen-year-old self again, trailing after her brother's friend with puppy dog eyes, hoping he'd notice her. And Joel had—well, not in a romantic sense. But she didn't want that, did she? Of course she didn't. She couldn't entertain the thoughts of a future with a man like Joel. Friendship. That was all she wanted.

Friendship. She'd have to keep repeating that to herself, especially when he smiled at her the way he was right now. Her heart somersaulted beneath her rib cage, but that was probably because she was nervous about the motorcycle ride.

Chapter Seven

Shelby glanced at the people talking to each other in the square. In less than a minute, they'd see Joel and her take off on his bike. What would they think of little Shelby Beck doing such a thing? Probably that she was out of her mind.

Stop worrying what others would think.

Joel said she needed to take some safe risks to liven up her days and he was right. Through the years, circumstances beyond her control had come into her life, and they had been rough to deal with—the fire, Dad leaving, Mom's quickly lost battle with cancer, and then Caleb's wife, Sarah, passing away. Because of those events, the rest of her life—every aspect that she could control—had been safe. No waves. No boat rocking. She'd lived with Caleb, had decided to turn down her chance to go to college and stayed tucked away in Goose Harbor.

Only now she was beginning to see what using the excuse of security to avoid taking chances had cost her.

What had become of her childhood dreams of traveling? Of seeing the Rockies and visiting Australia someday? She'd made herself believe the risks of going on those long-wished-for adventures outweighed the joy of the journeys. But now she wasn't so sure.

Joel handed her a black-and-red helmet. "Go ahead and put this on."

"Where's yours?"

"That is mine." He pressed it into her hands.

"Shouldn't you wear it?" She offered it back to him.

He took the helmet and lifted it over her head. "I'm more concerned with you being safe than me. Besides, if something did go wrong, you have people to miss you. I don't."

That wasn't right of him to say. She wanted to correct him and tell him she'd miss him. But that would cause another awkward moment between them. And how could she miss him when she didn't know him? Honestly, in the past fourteen years he hadn't crossed her mind except for a couple of times. Somehow, the past week had changed that. If Joel did leave again, Shelby's mind would wander to thoughts of him often. Hopefully that wouldn't happen.

She held her hair together at the nape of her neck while he eased the helmet onto her head and fastened the strap.

"It's probably a little big on you, but it's better than nothing."

Shelby felt silly. Were people staring? Her fingertips found the ends of the sleeves of the coat she wore, and she tugged down the fabric as far as it would go over her hands. Did the helmet make her look as ridiculous as she felt?

"Stop fidgeting. It's a good look on you. Cute. I promise." Joel swung onto the bike. "Go ahead and get on."

"I don't know what I'm doing. What if I do it wrong?" No longer doing somersaults, her heart jackhammered against her ribs. Her throat went dry. This was stupid. How had Joel tricked her into doing something so dangerous? People died in motorcycle accidents. Although, she supposed, they died doing mundane things, too.

Stop worrying. She could do this. Something small. Something out of her control.

"I'm going to teach you. Trust me. That's all I ask." He held out his hand. "Come with me, Shelby." His voice was low and his eyes searched hers. "Go ahead and get on the bike." She took his hand and stepped closer. "Now when you lift your leg over the seat, find the peg on the side of the bike. That's where your foot goes. There's one on each side."

Following his instructions, she swung her leg over. She grabbed Joel's shoulders to steady herself as she found the pegs for her feet. It felt as if the bike was going to tip over at any moment. "Are you sure two people can be on here?"

"Positive." He twisted in the seat to make eye contact. "You're doing great."

"I'm just sitting."

"There are only two things you need to do and you've already mastered the first. See? This is easy."

"What's the second?"

"Hang on."

"Where do I put my hands?" She fumbled to find a handhold on the seat. How fast would the bike go? What if she fell off the back? "I don't think I can hold on tight enough." Her voice faltered.

Joel acted like he hadn't heard her, even though he must have. "You have two options. Just behind the bike's taillight you'll find two handles. You can hang on there."

Again, she grabbed Joel's shoulder to steady herself as she found the handles. They were so far back. She'd have to be almost to the very edge of the seat to get a good grip. "I can't do this. I don't feel safe. What's my other option?"

"Hold on to me."

"You won't mind?"

"Not one bit."

"Where will I...?"

"You'll lean into my back, wrap your arms around my waist and keep your hands under my arms." He held her gaze. There were only inches between them. "Honestly, it's easier for me to balance the bike if you hold on to me and not the handles."

"Okay. Since that's better for you."

"When we're going, follow my body moments as much as you can. When we take a curve you'll want to fight what I'm doing, but don't. We'll lean into the turns, and it'll feel scary at first because your brain tells you to lean against the turn, but if you do that it can throw off our balance and make me lose control of the bike."

She swallowed. "Maybe I shouldn't do this."

"You'll be fine. We won't go far this first time."

"But I don't want to topple the bike."

"Shelby." His voice was soft and warm. "You're not going to do anything wrong. Not as long as you trust me. Do you trust me?"

"You'd never hurt me."

"That's my girl. Let's go, then."

He shoved up the kickstand with his foot and the bike rumbled like an angry lion. Her feet vibrated on the pegs, and she clenched her teeth as she adjusted to the feel of the engine. She wound her arms around his sides and fisted her hands into the fabric of his T-shirt. Joel nodded to her, leaned forward and then the bike moved out into traffic.

A part of her wanted to look around while they rode, and maybe she'd work up the courage, but at the beginning, she scooted as close to Joel as she could and laid the side of her head against his shoulder. Heat radiated off his skin through the thin cotton T-shirt. The side of her left hand pressed against the steady thump of his heart.

At first, they traveled slowly because they were still in the residential part of town, but the moment the bike cleared the limits of Goose Harbor, Joel turned them onto one of the many country roads that lined the shores of Lake Michigan and kicked the bike into a higher speed. Wind whipped at her clothes as she clutched Joel's shirt even tighter. The fabric would probably be stretched out when they returned to town.

After a few minutes, she lifted her head from his shoulder and tried to take in the view while still leaning with him on the bike. Sand dunes, small homes and patches of tall trees flashed by. Lake Michigan was a blur of blue on her left and a vineyard a blur of green on her right.

Joel leaned into a sharp curve and Shelby instantly realized what he meant about her head telling her to lean against it. She fought the desire and leaned into the turn with Joel and started to laugh. Had she been smiling the entire time? More than likely. If it had been safe to, she would have tossed her arms out to the sides and let the wind rush against her. She'd never felt so free in all her life. It was exhilarating. No wonder Joel loved this.

The ride didn't last nearly long enough. Fifteen minutes later, Joel slowed the bike down as they entered the residential part of town.

At a stop sign, he turned and leaned back into her. "What did you think?"

His face was inches from hers. Shelby's vision raked over his warm hazel eyes, the slant of his tanned nose and then landed on his lips. "I loved it."

"I hoped you would." He twisted back around and put the bike on course to deposit her on the doorstep of Gran's Candy Shoppe. Joel dropped her off, but waited to leave until she was safely upstairs in her apartment.

It was only after she heard the rumble signaling he was leaving that she noticed she still wore his leather coat.

Despite the warmth of the day, it tended to get pretty chilly by the lake in the evening. At home, Joel searched for his coat until he remembered Shelby still had it. No matter. He tossed on a hooded sweatshirt while Dante danced and whined around his feet.

"Just a minute, boy. Your walk's coming." He jammed his feet into his shoes and clipped the leash on to his dog's collar.

Dante had a way of wiggling his whole body back and forth when he was excited. He butted up against Joel's legs and looked up at him, his tongue hanging out the side of his mouth.

"You goof." Joel ruffled the fur on top of the dog's head and then opened the front door.

His dog might have been old and have joint problems,

but that didn't stop Dante from plowing ahead when they went for walks. Especially late at night like this when nocturnal animals came out. Joel shoved a stick of cinnamon gum into his mouth and watched Dante for signs of pain because, left to his own devices, the dog would push through any discomfort.

A few days ago, Joel scoped out trails in the area and had found one that started at the end of his street and wove through a small wooded area, which led to the beach. He steered Dante down the trail, letting the dog stop and smell whatever he wanted. Dante was cooped up in the house most days so he deserved as many sniffs as he could get on their walks.

At the beach, Joel eased out of his shoes. His bare feet slapped the wet sand along the shoreline. Without intending to, his mind wandered over the past week and a half. One particular face kept popping into his mind. *Shelby's.*

It had felt good—more than good—to have her draped across his back as they'd sped down a long, winding road. She was the kind of person who'd always been missing from his life. Sweet, positive, loyal, trusting. And she believed in him.

She was unattached, but a woman like Shelby wouldn't stay single for long. He'd heard the men at the coffee shop the first time he and Shelby had gone out. They'd dated her and had missed out. They only said cruel things because of hurt egos, and their pride wouldn't have been hurt so much if they hadn't wanted their relationships with Shelby to work. If Joel didn't make a move soon, someone else would.

Sure, he'd told himself not to get involved, but not getting involved could make him miss out on something amazing. So why hang back? Perhaps, as long as no one figured out the truth about him, Joel could have all his dreams.

"Who's there?" someone called from the direction of the parking lot above the beach.

Joel stopped and squinted, trying to make out the owner of the voice. It sounded familiar. "Miles?"

"Oh, hey, Joel." In uniform, Miles skidded down a small dune instead of taking the steps and joined Joel. "What are you doing on the beach so late?"

"Walking my dog." He dangled the leash. "Is that a crime in these parts?"

"No." Miles fell into step with him. "I just saw movement and wanted to check it out because we've had a lot of trouble with juveniles coming down here for drinking parties after curfew."

"If it helps, I haven't seen anyone."

"Well, that's good. Do you mind if I walk with you for a few minutes?"

"Last I checked it's a free country, Officer." Joel laughed. Cops made him uncomfortable. Even Miles. But, tonight at least, he had nothing to hide.

Miles nodded once and kept pace with Joel and Dante. What could his old friend want? Joel glanced at Miles. Cops didn't just go for strolls while they were on shift. The officer had to be up to something, or investigating him for who knew what reason.

Miles finally cleared his throat. "I'm worried about Shelby."

Shelby? Here it came. Caleb probably sent Miles to give him a stern talking-to. Joel decided to play along in the beginning just to see what Miles would say. "Worried?"

"Did she tell you she met with a construction company the other day?"

"She didn't." A hollow feeling settled in Joel's gut. It bothered him that she hadn't mentioned anything. But then, why would she?

"Well, she signed a contract with the first company she spoke to about the church plan and—this is between you and me—I have a long history back at the station regarding the owner and his employees, and the scams they have run. I've received some warnings from other nearby departments, as well."

Joel stopped walking. "Scams?"

"Shoddy work and plenty of corners cut." Miles turned to face Joel. "The owner is smart, though. He flirts right on the line of legal and illegal activity, which means I haven't been able to convince the county prosecutor to let me seek a warrant on him yet."

Joel's hand fisted around Dante's leash, and he commanded his muscles to relax. "You can't let them work on the church, then. This project means a lot to Shelby."

"I know. It's a shame. I wish I could have prevented her from working with them, but it was too late by the time she told me, and she never even consulted Caleb. Which is out of character for her." Miles shrugged.

"Why don't you just tell her all of this?"

"I shouldn't be telling you any of it, let alone her. All of this information is from confidential police reports. I could get in trouble for what I'm telling you right now. Best to keep my eye on the company and catch them before anything goes too wrong with the church."

"You should at least tell Caleb."

Miles laughed once. "Her overprotective brother? Not likely. Listen, Caleb is my best friend, but if I told him he'd barrel at these guys ten minutes later and blow my investigation."

"But I don't want Shelby hurt."

"Well, it's a good thing you're helping with the re-build. You can stick close to her and make sure she's safe."

Joel had only planned on assisting her with the fundraiser. Being on-site while the church was built was not something he wanted to do. But if he avoided it and the men conned Shelby, he'd never forgive himself.

So much for steering clear of the church.

Chapter Eight

Shelby ran her pen down the to-do list for the fundraiser as Caleb carried the last box of supplies to his pickup truck. Since she was carless for the time being, he'd been kind enough to lend her his truck for the evening.

Would she and Joel be able to finish everything tonight? They'd have to.

Caleb snapped the tailgate back into position. "Are you sure you don't want me to come to help unload and set up everything? I wouldn't mind."

Her brother asking to go either meant Paige had plans and he had nothing to do tonight, or he was concerned about Shelby for some reason. Perhaps he thought she was stressed about the event. Sure, she was. But she didn't need her big brother trying to rescue her anymore. Not from stress—not from anything.

"No way." Shelby slipped her notebook into her bag. "Enjoy your last Friday night as a single man."

The truck keys rested in his hand. "I'll still be single next Friday."

"Wedding's next Saturday buddy. So your rehearsal is on Friday."

"Which I'll still be single at."

Shelby fought an eye-roll. "Okay. Tonight's your last *free* Friday. You know how it goes. From that moment you say *I do*, your time is spoken for. Go play basketball with the guys or something."

"I'm not really the go-out-and-celebrate-your-last-bit-of-singleness type of guy. I can't wait to marry Paige. You know that. Speaking of it, Paige probably wouldn't mind meeting us at the firehouse to help out tonight, either." He pulled his cell phone from his pocket.

Shelby laid her hand over his phone to stop him from dialing. "No. You are both already helping with the event tomorrow, so let her relax tonight. Or go bring her flowers. Something besides spending the night decorating for a pancake breakfast."

He searched her eyes. "We wouldn't mind."

"You said that already." Why was he looking at her like that? As if he was trying to figure out a puzzle?

"Because it's true"

Okay. Hard to believe, but he was being more persistent than usual, which needed to stop because she'd told Joel she'd meet him an hour ago.

Shelby crossed her arms over her chest. "Out with it."

"With what?"

"I know you too well, Caleb." She stepped closer, just to let him know she wasn't intimidated by him the way she used to be. "You have a reason for wanting to come along, and it has nothing to do with helping me work. How about instead of talking in circles for the next ten minutes, you just tell me what's going on."

"You're right. There is something more." He looped

his hand around the back of his neck. "I don't know how to say this—"

"How about simply spitting it out?"

"It's Joel."

Joel? What about him? Caleb couldn't think that she and Joel… "Care to expand?"

"I don't like you two getting close and spending so much time together alone."

She tried to read the meaning behind what Caleb had just said. Was he upset she'd spent time with Joel and not him? Or that Joel hadn't sought out Caleb's friendship during his free time? Either way, her best option was to make a joke. Maybe then Caleb would loosen up or let go of whatever was dogging him.

"Aw. I never took you for the jealous type."

His voice rose a notch. "Could you be serious about this for a minute?"

Wrong thing to say.

"Sorry." Her mouth went dry. Caleb didn't get upset with her very often. "I guess I don't understand what you're saying or why you're upset."

"We don't know him. Not well. It might be better to keep your distance."

"I don't understand. He's your friend."

"Fourteen years ago, you'd be correct. Today—" he shrugged "—I have no clue who he is right now, but so far I'm not impressed. He keeps to himself so much, and I know for a fact he skipped church last week. He takes you out on a motorcycle. You know how many people get killed on those machines?"

Shelby crossed her arms. "Perhaps Joel's not out to impress you."

"What I know about him isn't great. He left here

without a trace. All I know is he took off to Indiana, and I don't even know if that's true. How can we believe what he says?"

"You're seriously not making any sense. Did you already forget that you've invited him to your wedding?"

"That was before he started cozying up to my sister. I have a bad feeling about him that I can't explain. It's a gut thing. Besides, even when he lived here before, he might have been my friend, but he was bad news."

She couldn't believe what Caleb was saying. It was so out of character for him. Caleb usually spent his time encouraging the best out of people. Not ripping them down. There had to be more to his doubts about Joel than he was voicing. Did she want to know?

No. She'd choose to hope for the best.

"I can't believe you. If this is how you talk about your old friends, I'd love to see how you talk about people you don't like."

Caleb crossed his arms. "Did he or did he not take you out for a ride on his motorcycle?"

Her brother knew about that? Well, of course he did—practically the entire town had seen them at the square. She swallowed hard. "What does that matter?"

"Answer my question."

"He did." Shelby raised her chin.

Caleb's eyes widened. "Do you have any concept of how dangerous that is?"

"Yeah, actually I do. And know what? I loved it. If Joel offers to take me again, I'll say yes."

"Don't." Caleb shook his head. "Please, don't."

"I'm not a child, Caleb. When are you going to see that?"

"When you stop acting like one." At least he winced after he said that.

Shelby spun away from him.

He placed his hand on her shoulder and gently turned her around. "You're the only family I have. I don't want to see you hurt in any way."

Joel's challenge in the laundry room came back to her. He'd been right. Because of Caleb's overprotection, she had never lived life. Not really.

Shelby shrugged away from her brother's touch. "I'm sick of a safe life. I'm so tired of never taking any risks. I want to get on that bike and take off for Colorado and see the mountains. I want to jump on a plane tomorrow and head to London. I want to live. Is that so bad?"

"Those are nice dreams, but perhaps Joel's not the man to have them with. Not yet anyway. Let's wait until we know who he is now better." He spoke softly, probably trying to calm her down.

"What's the point? No one will ever live up to what you want them to be." Her eyes burned with tears she tried to keep in. She gestured behind her, showing no one was waiting around. "I don't exactly have a string of men hoping to spend time with me. You've seen to that most of my life and scared them all away." She stopped him coming any closer by putting up her hand. "So far from what I can tell, Joel enjoys spending time with me. It won't last forever—*it can't*. But let me enjoy being his friend for now, okay?"

"I can't."

"Why won't you let me be happy? What's so wrong with that?" She swiped hot angry tears from her cheeks. Now her face would be red and blotchy when she arrived at the firehouse. Great.

"Shelb, I want you happy. I want that most in the world. But trust me on this, Joel has a bad background and you don't want to bring that into a relationship." Caleb raised both hands to keep her from butting in. "Let's say that, besides the bike, he's an upstanding guy now. Even so, he's a bad match for you because he grew up without parents. He's never had the opportunity to watch a married couple that loves each other and learn from them. He hasn't had a man in his life who's taught him how to treat a woman right or how to be a good father. Because of all that, he'll never be a good match for any Christian woman."

How could Caleb hold Joel's childhood pain against him? Her brother's words made no sense.

"I can't believe you *of all people* would say something like that."

"Don't allow your heart to get involved with him. That's all I'm saying."

Caleb was used to having the last word in their conversations, but not this time. Not when he was acting so completely thickheaded. "You can't hold his past against him."

"You have to if you care about your future."

"So tell me, are you planning on walking out on Paige someday?"

"I'd never." He stepped back as if he'd been struck. "Why would you say something like that?"

"I mean, Dad walked out on Mom. So, by your logic, you'll end up doing the same to your wife."

"It's not the same. At all."

"But it is."

"Hear me out. I just have this feeling that—"
Enough!

"I've listened to you my whole life, and where has that gotten me? Safe in Goose Harbor." She touched his arm. "I don't blame you. I can only imagine what you felt and went through when you had to take over as man of the family, and then only years later, lost your first wife in such a violent way."

She hated bringing up Sarah's death. No man should lose his young wife. She'd died so senselessly, shot outside the nonprofit she'd started to help inner-city teens in the troubled town of Brookside.

Shelby sucked in a fortifying breath. "But I'm done letting your worry control me. Yes, you've gotten better about it. Tons better because Paige keeps you in check. But you need to stop telling me what I can and can't do anymore, because I'm not listening."

"Shelby."

"I'm late. Give me the keys." She held out her hand.

He placed the keys in her palm.

She closed her fingers around the metal and then swung open the truck's front door. She and her brother never fought. Not like this. But he was wrong about Joel. Still, she couldn't leave Caleb thinking she was so angry she wouldn't speak to him. If the fire all those years ago had taught her one thing, it was that life could change in an instant. If something terrible happened, she'd never want a fight to be their last memory together.

Shelby glanced back. "Have a good night."

He'd slipped off his baseball cap and bent the bill between his hands. "I love you."

"I know. You, too." She sighed. "And I'm not mad at you, but I do think you need to search your heart some, because you're judging Joel pretty harshly right now."

Before he could restart the conversation, she hopped

into the truck. In a rush now, she didn't bother adjusting the seat and mirrors. She sat on the edge of the seat so her toes reached the pedals. Good enough.

Joel checked his watch again.

Shelby hadn't called to let him know she'd be running late and hadn't answered any of his calls or texts. If something had happened to her—he'd know, right? The firehouse would have been dispatched to an emergency. *Stop thinking of the worst possible scenario.*

Although, when he'd first arrived in town, he'd run into her because she'd just hit a deer. So maybe wondering if she had been in an accident wasn't so off base.

Joel stretched to work out the kinks in his shoulders. He prowled to the picnic table near the front of the station but then paced away from it.

She was fine. She would have called, wouldn't she have? No. Shelby would have called her brother. Someone at the firehouse must have Caleb's number. He started for the building but stopped when he heard a truck rumbling down the road. He spotted a tiny woman barely visible over the dashboard.

Joel was at the driver's window before Shelby had time to shut off the truck. He hooked his hand on the edge of the door near her elbow. "You, my dear, are late."

"Sorry. Blame my brother." She jammed the vehicle into Park and didn't look at him.

"No worries. I was kidding."

"I know. Sorry—"

"No more saying sorry tonight. You've already met your quota of two apologies for the day, and it's only been about forty seconds." He popped open her door as she gathered her purse. "Let's get these boxes out and go inside."

He hauled out the largest box. As he eased it out of the truck's bed, he looked inside. It held some cooking supplies for the pancakes and a bunch of boxes of frozen breakfast sausages.

Shelby grabbed a small box of decorations and followed him to the building.

Joel glanced back at her. Her brows were drawn low. Whatever she was thinking about couldn't have been good because her lips were pressed tightly together to form a grim line.

Distraction could be his ally, at least until she wanted to talk.

"I already cleared out the garage area and swept it. I got some of the guys to help me set up tables and chairs, and we washed the fire engines so they'll sparkle for the crowd tomorrow."

"You didn't have to do all that work." Setting down her box on the closest round table, she surveyed the open garage.

Unlike a regular car garage, the fire station was clean. No spilled oil or stains on the floor. The room was large with a high ceiling to accommodate the fire trucks. Tomorrow, as long as the weather cooperated, they'd leave the massive doors open. There were enough seats to fit about a hundred people.

"It didn't take long to set up," Joel said.

Shelby's fingers laced together. "Do you think we put up enough signs? What if people don't know about the breakfast?"

So, she was just nervous about the event.

He chuckled. "We put a sign on every corner in town.

Everyone knows. They'll be here. Tell me what you want me to do and we'll get started."

"There are a lot more boxes to carry in." She jutted her thumb toward the truck.

"As you wish." He winked at her. It took him ten minutes to carry everything in.

She had boxes and boxes full of little churches, which she'd built out of Popsicle sticks and painted white. Each one had a small slit in the top where people could drop donations inside. They looked just like the old chapel. Joel busied himself with putting away all the food in the kitchen area while Shelby carefully took out the churches and placed one at the center of every table. Next, she began setting up other decorations.

Whenever he walked into the room, she stopped what she was doing and watched him.

"What else do we have left to do?"

"Not much." She shrugged and continued hanging signs where they would set up the silent auction in the morning.

He'd expected her to be happy. Hadn't she told him rebuilding the church was her dream?

Joel shoved his hands into his pockets and cleared his throat. "Is something wrong?"

She stared at the ground, and tugged on her sleeves until they covered her hands entirely.

He inched closer. "You can tell me anything. You know that, right?"

"Caleb says I should stay away from you." Her eyes widened, almost as if she hadn't expected to say that out loud.

For a moment, her words became a vise around his throat. What could Joel say? He'd counted Caleb as a friend, and he'd been wrong. One more person who'd only pretended to care about him. Did Caleb still hold the same sway over what Shelby did and didn't do? Joel needed to find out.

He dragged in a deep breath through his nose. "I guess what matters most to me is what you think about that."

"Are you mad?"

More disappointed. He shrugged. "Caleb's allowed to think whatever he wants. Either way, I don't want to cause division between you two. Family's important to me."

"If you don't want to spend time with me anymore because of that, I understand." She studied the floor.

The slump of her shoulders propelled him forward. He ran his fingers down her arms and took hold of her hands, which caused her to look up and make eye contact.

"I like spending time with you. I want to keep seeing you and getting to know you more. But that's all up to you and what you feel comfortable with. Like I said, I don't want to be the cause of a rift with your brother, but if I can do something to make him feel better about it, I'm more than willing."

"I shouldn't have told you, but I felt like you deserved to know."

"Tell me whatever you want." Images flashed in his mind. A captured moment of his mother yelling at him for dropping a toy on the ground, followed by another of a father from one of his foster families telling him he'd never be good enough. "It's okay. Believe me, I've been told my faults many times and lived."

"But that's just it—it's not your fault. Caleb is being

thick-skulled. He says I shouldn't get close to you because of your past."

Joel's heart pounded in the back of his throat. Did Caleb know about the church? He licked his lips. "My past?"

"Growing up in foster homes and being taken from your mom. Everything you've been through."

"We can't hang out together because I was a foster kid?" He let go one of her hands and rubbed his brow. "I don't understand."

"He said you won't know how to treat a woman. He said—"

Joel squeezed the hand he still held. "Know this, Shelby. I'd never, ever intentionally hurt you. Now, I can't promise that if we keep getting to know each other you'll like everything about me. I might have habits that annoy you, and someday I may say something that unintentionally hurts you. If I've learned one thing in life, it's that people hurt other people, whether we mean to or not. I'll try my hardest to never cause you pain, and someday when I do, I'll do everything in my power to make it right."

He placed her hand on his chest, and rested both of his hands over hers. Their faces were now less than a foot apart. "So, there you have it. I'm far from perfect. Very far, if I'm being honest. But if you want to, I'd love to keep getting to know you and spending time together."

"I want that, too," she whispered.

"Then how about a walk on the beach?"

She nodded and smiled. As he led her out of the firehouse, he couldn't help but wonder what their conversation meant from Shelby's point of view. Had they just decided to start dating? If so, he'd better prepare for another visit from Caleb.

Chapter Nine

The firehouse sat on top of a sloping cliff on the edge of the downtown portion of Goose Harbor that ran parallel to the lake. While the town square was closer to the waterline, the fire department had been built up the hill a ways, sitting above the rest of the buildings.

Joel laced his fingers with Shelby's and led her around the back of the station to a long path of stairs down to the beach. A small forest grew along the sandy cliff side, slowly thinning out closer to the shore. The cold lake breeze brought out the sweet smell of the evergreens. On a slow workday, Joel and the other firefighters would need to trim some of the low hanging limbs on the path.

Shelby grabbed the wooden railing as she ducked under a large branch. "I didn't realize how steep it was here."

He squeezed her hand. "I've got you."

"No way. If I fall, you're going to tumble right along with me." She laughed.

"EMT, remember? We'll be fine."

"Not if I take us both out, which I'm liable to do."

"Well, if you trip, just push me down first and I'll pad your fall."

"I'll try to keep that in mind."

As they navigated the narrow flight of stairs, his hip bumped against hers. Joel caught her as she wobbled a bit. "Steady."

"I'll be fine as long as you stop shoving me." She playfully elbowed his side.

How long had it been since Joel had been able to laugh and joke around with someone? Years, if he was being honest. In his last position as a hotshot firefighter, he helped fight raging forest fires. The job had been too stressful for the sort of male bonding that led to teasing and laughter. When staring into the face of a seven-hundred-acre inferno, becoming buddies with the guy next to him had been the last thing on his mind.

Survival. It was a recurring theme in his life, and it had won out over friendship. Anyway, friendship meant talking to people, spilling guts and feelings, and discussing unhealed hurts. Things Joel prided himself on not doing. He hadn't wanted the other guys to consider him weak, and that was what his past said. Cast-off. Unwanted. No good.

Even before then, when he worked near Indy and Charlie Greave mentored him, their relationship had been serious and purposeful. They'd never gotten together just to shoot the breeze or watch the game. That just hadn't been the basis of their friendship. Charlie had been a mentor, nothing more, nothing less.

Walking beside Shelby felt different than all his prior relationships, because she made him feel at ease. That was something of a rarity in his life.

He could laugh with her one minute and the next,

tell her something that had been weighing on his mind. She usually opened up pretty quickly about what she was thinking. When she didn't, the emotions on her face were easy to read.

Perhaps it was her compassionate spirit that drew his attention. Whatever the reason, he was thankful. He'd forgotten how *freeing* it was to smile.

Maybe he'd never known.

At the bottom of the stairs, they both removed their shoes and tucked them under the final step for safe keeping until they returned. Shelby shivered when her bare feet touched the cool sand. Side by side, they started north along the beach. Their feet made the trademark squeaking sound as they walked thanks to the high quartz content in the sand along the shores of Lake Michigan. Joel had been gone almost long enough to forget the sound.

The dim, pink line of sun on the horizon would disappear completely within the next fifteen minutes, but the glow from Goose Harbor provided enough light for them to navigate the beach. He steered her away from the patches of dune grass that grew next to the boardwalk and led her close to the waterline.

"I forgot how big of a temperature drop there is near the water when sun goes down. Do you want my coat?" He shrugged out of the fleece jacket he'd pulled on before they'd left.

Shelby shook her head. "No, thanks. I already have one of your coats hostage back at my place. If I take another, you'll quickly find you have none left."

"Are you sure?" He held it out to her. "I wouldn't mind."

"Positive. I have on two layers already and long

sleeves. I'm fine. I just wasn't expecting the sand to be so cold already after how warm it was out today."

Long sleeves again, which worked well for their unplanned stroll, but she had to have been pretty warm while they had been setting up for the pancake breakfast. In fact, he'd noticed since returning to Goose Harbor she always wore long pants and long sleeves. That was her right, but the unexpected warm start to summer made him wonder if Shelby had a reason for wearing what she did.

"I've noticed…" Maybe it wasn't for him to know.

"Yes?"

Joel cleared his throat. "You wear long sleeves all the time. I wondered why."

Shelby stopped walking and faced the lake's still water. She crossed her arms and rubbed her hands up and down her arms as if she was cold. The set of her shoulders told him she was upset. She tilted her head so she could look up at the stars. Was she trying to keep from crying?

He fought the urge to put his arms around her. Instead, he stepped so he was beside her and looked out at the lake. "Sorry. I shouldn't have said anything."

"No, it's okay. I just…" She palmed her cheek.

Seeing her cry hurt ten times worse than getting clocked in the jaw would have. He never again wanted to be the cause of her tears. "Forget my big mouth. You don't have to say anything."

She sucked in a shuttered breath. "I should tell you. It'll come out eventually. Foolishly, I just hoped it wouldn't be so soon."

Stop her tears, dumb man. He needed to help her by filling in the words so she wouldn't have to.

"Is it a modesty thing? If so, I think that's great. Too many women parade around with far too much skin showing." He was rambling, which wasn't like him, but he wanted to take away her pain. "Know what? I used to know someone who was allergic to sunlight. He had to wear a hat at all times to shade his face. Is it something medical like that?"

"A mix of both." She shrugged and started walking again.

Joel fast-stepped to keep up with her pace. He decided to keep his mouth closed.

She stopped again and faced him. "We never talk about you."

That escalated fast. "We talk about me all the time."

"Not really."

"What do you want to know?" Please ask about the fire department. Or Dante. Or motorcycles. Anything but—

"Tell me about your past."

Buy time.

He swallowed hard as he turned and explored the beach for a stone. A pebble would have to do. Joel scooped it up and launched it into the lake. "Probably because there isn't much to tell."

"You know what?" She moved a couple of steps away and then studied him. "This is what Caleb was talking about. He's right that we don't know much about the person you are now."

"What am I supposed to say?" He balled his hands. "Everything that's happened to me isn't worth repeating."

"Trust me," she whispered. "How come you won't trust me?"

"Shelby, believe me when I say I've known you less than a month and I already trust you more than any other person in my life."

"Then fill me in. I can only get as close to you as you'll let me."

Precisely the problem. Did he want a close relationship like she did? Sure, he enjoyed spending time with her, liked hearing her talk about her life and she made him smile like he hadn't in a long time. But were those things worth the pain that more than likely would accompany the moment she decided she was done with him? It had never been worth it with any of his foster families. Not one.

Shelby looked like she was going to start crying again, and he'd just promised himself he wouldn't be the cause of her tears anymore. He needed to say something.

He cleared his throat. It still felt as dry as the brush that started wildfires. Why was this so difficult? "I...I don't want you to look at me differently."

"I won't."

"*You will.* Everyone does." Once people heard about sad little Joel Palermo, they all got the same look: that cartoon-eyes-welling-up-with-tears face, their expressions a clear mix of wondering if they should hug him or step away slowly.

"Maybe we should go back."

He caught her arm. "Stay. Please." Joel's eyes searched hers.

She licked her lips. "Give me a reason to stay."

Joel automatically leaned closer. The lights from town made Shelby's pale skin almost glow in the darkness. She was such an amazing woman, and he wanted her to know how much he cherished spending time with her, but he'd never been good with words.

Testing the waters, he let go of her arm and brought his hand to cradle the back of her head. His thumb lightly brushed the soft skin where her neck and jaw met. Shelby tilted her head up, and their noses grazed. Their lips met, softly and for only a few seconds, but that's all it took to feel as if someone had lit off a firework in Joel's stomach.

He broke contact with her. What was he doing? She'd just asked for something personal from him. A shared kiss might appease her tonight, but later on when she thought back over the evening, it would appear to be a distraction to throw her off of her original desire—knowing his heart.

"I'm sorry. I shouldn't have done that." Joel paced away, wondering if her heart was pounding as hard as his.

"You…you didn't like that?" Shelby tugged at her sleeves.

Joel rushed back to her and clasped both her hands. "I liked it. More than I can say. But you asked me to talk about myself, and I don't want you to think I kissed you to avoid that. What do you want to know about my past?" As long as she didn't ask why he left town.

"Whatever you want to share."

"I'm going to be honest with you. Because I never had a home or a family, I have a really hard time talking about personal stuff—the deeper stuff. I just…I don't know, it probably sounds stupid, but I always feel like people are going to leave me soon anyway, so way waste time and emotions digging up my past."

"Do you think I'm going to leave?"

"Nothing's ever certain."

She squeezed his hands and smiled up at him. "Some things are."

He turned her back in the direction of the firehouse. "Name them. But I'm taking Jesus off the table right now because I know He's the only certain thing in this life. We're talking earthly things."

"That's hard for me to answer, too," she said softly. "My parents divorced, so I can't say marriage is a sure thing, but I still believe in love that can last a lifetime because I've seen it. Here in town there is Ida Ashby. She's still devoted to her husband and he's been dead for years. Then I have Caleb and Paige."

"They're not even married yet, so we don't know what might happen."

"Oh, I do. Caleb and Paige are both committed to each other for life. There's no question about that."

"You're right. Some people do find friends who will stick by them no matter what. But I never have, and I probably don't deserve that anyway."

"Everyone deserves to be loved and cherished as is."

"Everyone? Do you really think that?"

"Everyone."

"So now I'm making you the doctor. Give me my diagnosis. How do we cure my inclination toward not trusting people or telling them about myself?"

"Each day you see me you have to tell me one personal thing about yourself."

"Only one?"

"That's all I'm asking for."

"One a day could take a really long time."

She bumped her shoulder against his. "I'm kind of hoping it does."

"Can I do my first one now?"

"I'm taking you telling me you don't like to open up as your one for the day, but you're always allowed to tell me as many as you want."

"Here goes. I like you Shelby Beck. I like you a lot."

Shelby's mind swirled as she tried to make sense of Joel's words and behavior. He was treating her like a girlfriend—and she was treating him like she wanted to start a relationship with him. And he'd kissed her. It hadn't been like any kiss she'd ever had. Joel's touch had made the rest of the world melt away. She had never experienced a moment like that. Ever.

Oh, no. What had she done?

She could never have a romantic relationship with Joel. His questioning her about her long sleeves only minutes ago confirmed it. It was only a matter of time before he found out about her scars.

And what had made her make him promise to tell her something deep about himself every day? Then tell him she hoped they'd share a close relationship long-term.

Shelby dragged her hands through her hair.

She was walking a dangerous line, because she also didn't want him to feel as if she was abandoning him the way he thought everyone else had.

Shelby, wake up!

Plain and simple, she was leading him on. Not in the way a girl did when she flirted with a guy she wasn't interested in. She would never do something like that. Every part of her desperately wanted a relationship with Joel. But who was she kidding? He would reject her the first time he saw her scars. And he would see them or find out about them eventually.

Was it possible to at least be good friends even after a kiss like the one they had shared? Hopefully.

Thankfully, they didn't talk on the way up the steep steps.

When they arrived at the top, she stepped out of his reach—just in case.

"I want you to know I'm happy for our friendship, too." There. That sounded like a civil, nonromantic statement. "We should head back. It's getting late and we both have to get up early tomorrow for the pancake breakfast."

Joel nodded. "Now that you've seen the finances in Mr. Ashby's account, do you think we'll raise enough tomorrow to fill the gap that you need?"

"I have faith the money will come through."

"Do you have more events planned in case you have to raise extra money? I'm not trying to be a downer, but sometimes you can have all the faith in the world and the thing you want to happen still doesn't."

Story of her life.

"It has to. We break ground on the church on Monday."

"Already?"

"I don't see a reason to delay."

"Have you checked into the company and contractor you're using?"

"They all seem nice enough."

"Would you mind if I stopped by the site and checked up on them? It's not that I don't think you can handle it, but I know a little about construction."

"I wouldn't mind at all. Will you be there Monday?"

"If I can make it there during a break, I will. I'm on shift then." They walked up the driveway to the station and the motion-sensor lights switched on. He stopped near her truck. "From what you've said, so much of your life is wrapped up in building the church. What will you do when it's done?"

Move on. Heal. Live. "Focus on something else."

"Now I'm the one asking for you to open up." He smiled. "I've listened to you talk about staying near Caleb in your life up until now, choosing not to go to college to stay in Goose Harbor, and about this church. But Caleb's getting married, Goose Harbor is changing and the church will be rebuilt. What then? You must have dreams."

"I'm not sure. I love working with dogs, but you're right. I've realized I probably shouldn't count on it forever if something as small as a car wreck can ruin my business. I guess…I don't know. Is that terrible?"

"Not terrible. Not at all. But it's something you need to start thinking about."

"I know." She scuffed her foot on the ground. "It's just…I'm having trouble knowing where to even start in the thinking process."

"God has given you a lot of talents. You're compassionate, loyal and you believe the best about people. But I think about the verse in the Bible where it says that to the person God gives a lot, a lot is required." He put his hand on her shoulder. "I'm encouraging you to spend some time with the Lord and search out what serving Him with your talents looks like in the future. That's all."

"You're a good man, Joel Palermo."

He gave her a half smile that didn't reach his eyes. "Drive safe and sleep well."

"You, too." She climbed into the truck and headed

off. In the rearview mirror, she saw Joel framed in the front door of the fire station, watching her drive away.

They could never be only friends, could they? Shelby's heart told her no, but her heart would just have to learn how to deal with it.

Chapter Ten

"I have a request for chocolate chip pancakes at table seven. Hold the sausage." Joel leaned against the counter and smiled at Maggie, who manned the stove top. Joel was relieved to have an excuse to sneak into the kitchen for a few minutes and duck away from the crowd. Sure, he was happy for Shelby. The room was packed, and there were even people who couldn't find seats. Her event would raise all the money she needed. But being in a large crowd would never make it on to his top-ten-favorite-things list. Not even close.

He glanced through the doorway and saw Shelby and one of the older firefighters trying to get the attention of the crowd so they could announce the winners of the silent auction.

Conversation mixed in a steady hum in the room behind him, and in the kitchen the sound of grease frying was only slightly louder than the four women who rushed around making food.

Maggie used the back of her hand to shove her big, curly hair behind her ear, leaving a splotch of pancake batter on her cheek. "Table seven? If I'm not mistaken, that's where the Holdens are sitting."

"Maybe." Joel shrugged. He'd been in town for close to a month, but he still didn't know most people by name.

"Of course it's the Holdens." Chief Wheeler's always-too-loud-voice made Joel jump.

Maggie nodded. "Then double helpings of chocolate chip pancakes coming their way."

Wheeler rested a hand on Joel's shoulder. "She would have done it for anyone, but the Holden children have seen a few rough years. The youngest was just declared cancer free. He deserves all the pancakes he can eat."

The youngest couldn't have been more than five or six years old. "I had no idea."

"You'd be surprised by some of the stories you don't know. There are plenty of people in this town who have been through great trials and pain in their lives. You're not alone when it comes to that. I hope you realize that, son. You are never alone. Communities exist to support the other members in the good—like today's event—and the bad, even when we bring about the bad ourselves." Wheeler's hand still rested on Joel's shoulder. Suddenly, it felt very heavy.

Is that the impression he'd given the chief? That he was weak and had suffered? He hoped not. "Somehow I think everyone's more eager to draw together for the good than when something bad happens."

Wheeler shook his head. "Then I'm afraid you don't know Goose Harbor well enough yet."

"Don't I?" He really should stop challenging his boss, but something about the large, always-smiling man reminded Joel of his old mentor, Charlie, and for a moment, he felt comfortable voicing his doubt.

Wheeler raised his eyebrows.

"Take the church, for example. Did the community come together after it burned down?" It wasn't the question Joel wanted to ask. *Would they forgive the man who burned it down?* But he knew the answer to that one and didn't want to hear it.

"They sure are now." The chief gestured to the over-flowing room.

"Yes, but why didn't they do this all those years ago? Why wait until now?"

"Because it wasn't the right time yet. You'll see. When this church breaks ground on Monday, it is going to heal a whole lot of people in this town."

"That's what Shelby keeps saying, but it doesn't make any sense."

Wheeler nodded. "Especially Shelby."

"Why do you say that?" Joel had tried to figure out why the church building meant so much to her, but had yet to come up with a reason.

"Sorry. You'll have to ask her yourself."

He would again, if he could catch her today. After their walk on the beach the previous night, Shelby fled home pretty quickly. Then this morning, she'd either been talking to someone or had been on the opposite side of the room from him whenever he looked for her. It was starting to feel as if she was avoiding him. Had the kiss scared her? Maybe she wasn't interested in him. What if she'd only pretended to like him—as Caleb and so many of his foster families had?

She's busy. Just busy.

Maggie slid a plate full of chocolate chip pancakes down the counter. "Who's bringing this to table seven?"

"Look lively." Wheeler shoved the plate into Joel's hands and slapped him on the back. "Make sure to show your pearly whites. Brooding has its place, but there are some lovely ladies out there who would fancy seeing a fireman waiting on them with a bright smile. Who knows, you just might get a few smiles back."

As instructed, Joel smiled as he dropped off the pancakes and then mingled with people at the next table, but it was for Shelby's sake, not because of the chief's ribbing. He wanted her event to be a success, and if that meant doing the rounds and laying on the fireman charm, he'd do it.

Even if the girl he was smiling for wouldn't make eye contact with him.

Shelby scanned the crowd and spotted Joel. He tossed his head back and laughed at something Bree, a schoolteacher about his age, said. Shelby clenched her teeth for a moment before forcing the muscles in her jaw to relax.

Hadn't she looked into her mirror at home and promised she'd only be friends with Joel? A friend had no reason to be jealous of his flirting with a cute, single schoolteacher. Yet the desire to go and tug him away from Bree's company was there. Was it so bad to want him to save his best smiles for her?

Paige appeared beside her and squeezed her hand. "He's pretty cute."

"Bree seems to think so."

"I wouldn't worry about Bree. I have it from the horse's mouth that she's sweet on the IT guy at school." Paige winked. Shelby had forgotten that Bree was

Paige's teaching buddy and they often spent time together outside school. Paige nudged Shelby in the side. "You know, he's really shown that he has a servant's heart with all the work he's done for this event. I can see why you like him."

"The IT guy?" Shelby knew Paige was talking about Joel, but didn't want to tip Paige off to her feelings. Not when Shelby's thoughts were so muddled and her heart hurt. If she started talking about him with her soon-to-be sister-in-law, she'd probably start crying, and that was the last thing she wanted to do, especially at the fund-raiser.

"Oh, please, I'm not blind." Paige gestured to indicate Joel.

Shelby snatched Paige's hand so people wouldn't see them pointing at him. "You think I like Joel? It's not like that."

"You've sure been spending a lot of time together. And Caleb told me about going for a motorcycle ride." Mischief danced in Paige's eyes. "Swoon."

"Ha. Caleb was mad I went."

"I hate to say this about my soon-to-be hubby, but I'm going to let you in on a secret. As wonderful as Caleb is and as much as we both love him, he's not always right."

"You can say that again."

Paige leaned in closer. "How about I repeat something else to you instead?"

"Why do I get the feeling I'm not going to like what you're about to say?"

"The day we picked up your bridesmaid dress, I said you needed to open yourself up to the possibility of a man loving you romantically. I still believe that. And if I'm not mistaken, Joel's already moving in that direction." Paige tilted her head to indicate where he stood helping a group of high school kids from the youth group fill glasses of orange juice to pass out.

She watched him for a minute as he chatted with the local teens, and her heart pounded harder. Had she really kissed him last night? Yes. And she wanted to again. It wasn't fair she had to give him up. He was exactly the guy she'd never let herself dare to dream about.

Shelby let out a breath. "You can't say something like that when you've never even talked to him."

"Sure I can. Anyone can tell, Shelb. The man hasn't stop watching you all day."

It was too much. She was going to start crying. If she couldn't get Paige to stop talking about Joel, at least they didn't need to do it in the firehouse.

Shelby grabbed Paige's hand and dragged her outside where no one could see them. "If I tell you something, you have to promise not to tell Caleb."

"I don't know…"

"Promise."

"Okay." Paige crossed her arms and raised her eyebrows. It was almost funny because the petite woman couldn't have looked intimidating if she had tried. "I won't tell our favorite overprotective bear."

"I kissed him. Joel. Joel and I kissed last night."

"Eek!" Paige lunged forward and wrapped Shelby in a tight hug. "I'm so happy for you. I haven't met him, but you know I've had a feeling about you two ever since Caleb told me Joel returned to town."

Shelby applied gentle pressure to get Paige to let her go. "But it can't be like that. You know I can't have that sort of relationship."

"Is this about what Caleb said the other day about

him? Because your brother and I talked that over and he knows he was out of line to say you shouldn't be around Joel because of his rough past. By that logic, Caleb and I shouldn't be getting married, because both of our parents had issues. Everyone does."

"No offense, but I wasn't listening to what Caleb said. I knew he was wrong."

"Okay—then I'm confused."

Shelby wrenched up her sleeve to show Paige the scar on her wrist. "What's it going to take for you and Caleb to understand that everything comes down to this?" She shook her arm at Paige. "Because of this, I have to live in heartache knowing there's a good man who cares about me and is interested in pursuing a relationship with me, but I have to turn him down. I have to exist in the same town, brushing shoulders with him knowing that if I didn't have these burns we could be dating. Maybe even be planning a life together down the road. But I can't. I'll never be able to. And I have to look him in the eye and tell him we can't be together, and then not give him a reason when he asks why."

Tears burned twin trails down her cheeks. She shoved down her sleeve and used the fabric to mop her face. "And it hurts. It hurts so much, Paige. I don't know if I can take it. I'm so tired of having to hide away my hopes and tell myself no. I didn't get a choice. That fire set a course for my life, and I never got a say in it. I didn't do anything wrong and it's like I'm being punished for the rest of my life. Why does God do this to us?"

"Shelby, it doesn't have to—"

Shelby swiped at her eyes. "You know, sometimes I feel like I shouldn't be involved in the church rebuild because, honestly, I still struggle with being angry at

God about the fire. Why did He let me go through that? I was a child and *I was praying.* I went there that day because I had faith He could make my life better, and it just made my life worse. Forever. Sometimes I get tired of having a brave face and acting like I'm okay. I'm not."

Paige's voice was soft when she spoke. "I'm afraid I don't have a good answer for you. There are so many things in this world I have questions about. Why does God let certain things happen? Like little Alex Holden in there—why did that tiny, sweet boy have to suffer through chemo? Why did Caleb have to go through losing his first wife in such a violent way when she was in the midst of serving people in need?"

Shelby nodded. Poor Caleb had lost his childhood sweetheart to a shooting; Sarah had been mentoring inner-city kids and trying to help them find a better future. But if she had lived, Paige wouldn't be standing in front of Shelby about to become her sister-in-law. Emotions could be so confusing. Shelby still mourned Sarah and wished Caleb hadn't had to experience such a loss. But she loved Paige and couldn't wait to have her in the family.

Paige laid her hand on Shelby's arm. "Why did you have to go through such pain and be left with these scars? I can't answer that for you. I don't think there *is* an answer because it wasn't a punishment, Shelby. All I know is that God grieved with you when you were in pain, and He wants to help heal you."

"The doctors say this is as healed as my skin will ever get." She dashed more tears from her face and looked up to try to get the waterworks to stop.

"Heal you in here." Paige tapped where her heart beat. "If you let Him, God wants to remove the scars from there most of all. He wants you to know with certainty that you are loved and you are whole and there is nothing lacking. Because of that, you shouldn't be afraid to let other people love you."

"If that beam hadn't fallen on me, I probably could have gotten out of the church without any burns. He could have prevented that from happening. All of it."

"Sadly, *what-ifs* don't solve anything. They just keep us up at night and fill our heads with lies about God. Nobody needs that." Paige pressed her lips together and then continued, "I might be speaking too boldly right now, but since you're not stopping me, I'm just going to say it."

Shelby shrugged. "You're fine. This is good stuff to hear. Caleb and the rest of the people who know have always coddled me and said they were sorry. I probably could have used a dose of tough love a long time ago."

"There's someone else who did nothing wrong and didn't deserve the suffering and intense pain he endured. He, too, questioned why God would make him experience such terrible circumstances, and begged God to take away his pain. I think you know I'm talking about Jesus. He understands your hurt and can handle your questions."

Shelby looked to her left and down the cliff toward the beach. Lake Michigan seemed to sparkle as the sun rose closer to the top of the sky. "In all the years I've been struggling with this, I never considered Jesus's suffering. So many people ask 'Why, God?' when bad things happen to them, but when it comes down to it, He was probably the only one with the right to ask that question since He never sinned. Even the one man who lived without sin suffered.

"Thank you, Paige. It doesn't take away my pain and confusion, but it does help to shift my perspective. I've been focusing on me and so worried about hiding from people that I haven't focused much on God, especially in the last couple of years."

"Glad to help. We can talk more about it anytime you want, okay?"

"Okay, but for now we should probably go help clean up. People are going to wonder where we've been."

Her future sister-in-law offered her arm and Shelby laughed and linked hers with Paige's. Hopefully, she didn't look quite the mess she felt she was, but either way, she whispered a prayer thanking God for bringing Paige into her life.

Joel stood by the front entrance to the firehouse directing traffic as people left the fund-raising event.

Where was Shelby? He hadn't spotted her in almost an hour, and the fire station wasn't a big enough place to lose somebody in. Maybe he'd check the kitchen again after he finished helping people leave safely.

"Hey, can I talk to you?" He didn't have to turn around to know the voice belonged to Caleb.

"I'm kind of busy right now." And Caleb had showed his true colors when he warned Shelby to stay away from Joel. Had she told her brother about the kiss? If so, then he really didn't want to talk to Caleb.

Joel kept his back to his old friend and flagged the next group of cars out onto the main road.

Caleb stepped into his line of vision. "It's important."

"So is directing traffic so people don't get into accidents."

"Which is why I brought a substitute. Lenny said

he'd take over until we're done talking. He helps direct traffic at all the school's football games, so I'm sure he can handle this." The man with Caleb held out his hand to take the flags from Joel. Lenny wore a collared shirt tucked into too-short shorts. Everything about him screamed gym teacher.

"Fine." Joel handed over the flags.

Neither he nor Caleb spoke as they trudged from the building to a spot on the side yard where no one could hear them.

Joel cleared his throat. "We both know you're going to tell me to keep away from your sister, so how about we cut our losses and save some time. I won't stop seeing her." He started to walk away.

"In fact, I was planning to say the opposite."

Caleb's admission stopped Joel in his tracks. "Opposite? But Shelby said you told her to steer clear of me."

"She told you what I said, huh?" He shuffled his feet and looked at the ground.

"She did."

Caleb pulled off his baseball hat and scrunched it between his hands. "Well, I'm sorry you had to hear that."

"It actually helps to know who my friends are and aren't."

"The truth is I'm not just sorry you had to hear that. It's more. I'm sorry I ever said or thought it. I pulled you aside now because I wanted to ask your forgiveness. No one deserves to be judged for a past they couldn't control, and I should be the first to know how those things can haunt you."

Joel blinked. No one had ever apologized for misjudging him. Ever. He didn't know how to respond, but it gave him hope. He took a step closer to Caleb so they didn't have to speak so loudly. "What about the parts of their past they could have controlled?"

"If we're going to judge a man, I say let's judge him based on who he is today and who he's working toward becoming tomorrow." Caleb jammed his hat back onto his head. "I was so concerned with not knowing everything about where you've been and why you left, that I didn't pay attention to who you are. Then I talked to Paige last night and watched you today. Joel, you're eager to help others. Your entire career is focused on serving people in the midst of traumatic situations. I don't know who you're striving to be tomorrow, but I trust it's someone who would hope for the best as far as Shelby's concerned."

A lump formed in Joel's throat. "I want only good things for her life."

Caleb nodded. "If you'll let me, I'd like to be your friend again. It's short notice, but I'd be proud if you would stand up in my wedding next Saturday. Paige said to let you know you're invited to the rehearsal the night before."

"I'm on duty this Friday. And I'd have to think about standing up." Joel rubbed the back of his neck.

"So no rehearsal. Even if you don't want to stand up, will you for sure come to the wedding?"

"I'll think about it and let you know."

Joel finally spotted Shelby, but she was climbing into a car with Paige. He wouldn't get to talk to her today. Yes, she'd been busy with the event, but after last night, the only thing that made sense was Shelby wasn't interested in him romantically. If she was, she would have found a reason to stay at the station a little longer or would have at least exchanged a "how are you?" with him at some point during the fund-raiser.

Perhaps hoping for the best for Shelby meant not including himself in the equation.

Chapter Eleven

Shelby stared at the contract in her hands. It might as well have been written in a different language.

She sighed in frustration. Thankfully, preliminary work on the church had started in the morning. The local gardening center had offered a worker and backhoe as a donation, but that only included general clearing of the land. Tasks that didn't involve the contractor.

She glanced at the contract again. While she had signed initial paperwork with the contractor, it seemed additions to the contracts were showing up daily. After church yesterday, she had been tempted to fess up to Caleb that she was in over her head, but then she remembered Joel's offer to help deal with the contractor.

He had said he'd stop by during a break from work today. However, after ignoring him at the fund-raiser on Saturday, Shelby wasn't so sure he'd make good on his promise. No calls yesterday and she hadn't spotted him around town. Although she could have called him and hadn't.

The contractor, who simply went by the name Pekin, crossed his arms over his large chest. His face was turned in her direction, but behind the wide sunglasses he wore, she couldn't tell where he was looking. "Have you about got those papers signed?"

"I'm still looking them over." If only she had a desk where she could fan out the inch-thick pile of papers and really read everything. He should have shown these to her at the office. Why had he sprung all this on her now?

He worked his jaw back and forth. "The church can't be built without those signed."

"I thought I signed everything already?"

"You signed saying you were going to work with my company. Not the specifics yet."

She tapped the top paper. "So these are all the specifics?"

He shrugged. "Most of them. Some stuff could come up along the way, and we'll talk then. That's how construction goes. Often we don't know until we get started." He pulled out his phone and walked a few paces away.

"Just let me look these over a bit more." She crossed the street to get away from all the dust caused by the backhoe's digging. She fished her phone from her bag and decided she needed Joel to see the paperwork before she signed anything.

She punched in a text:

I need help with the contractor. Are you able to stop by soon?

Maybe she should have started with saying she was sorry? Or hi. He might choose not to answer if he was angry.

Her phone pinged a moment later.

Be there in a few minutes.

Of course he would be. Since returning, Joel had always been quick to help. She shouldn't have doubted him. Tension vanished from her shoulders and she walked a block away from the building site. Joel would be able to spot her here and they could talk for a moment without the contractor overhearing.

Paige was right. Shelby needed to stop ruining relationships before the man involved had a chance to reject her. All that would do was leave her alone. Forever. And she didn't want that. Scary to consider, but she had to trust that Joel wouldn't judge her scars. If he did, she'd deal with the hurt then. She needed to stop imagining scenarios before they happened, and she had to open up her heart to the possibility of a long-term relationship with Joel—if she hadn't ruined everything already. *Please don't let that be true.*

She'd expected the rumble of a motorcycle, but spotted him driving one of the fire department's red SUVs instead. Right. He was still on duty and needed a fire vehicle in case he had to respond to an emergency.

He parked the vehicle and climbed out. The crisp white polo he wore boasted the department's logo embroidered over his heart. His last name was embroidered on the opposite side. Joel's black pants were pressed and his black work boots shone. Despite his sharp-looking uniform, lines circled Joel's eyes. His mouth drooped and flat hair spoke of either a sleepless night or a hard shift at work.

"It begins." Joel smiled, but it didn't reach his eyes.

"Well, it will after I sign all of this." She wagged the contract at him. "Thanks for coming so quickly."

"I told you I would."

"If it's too much trouble, I understand. But if you

have a minute, could you look this over for me and give me some advice?"

He whistled as he eased the paperwork from her hands. "That's quite a contract. It'll probably take more than a minute." Joel motioned for her to follow him to the SUV. He opened the rear and spread some of the pages out in the back of the vehicle. "I'm glad you called me. Listen, don't ever sign a contract unless you feel comfortable. Contracts always favor the writer, but all builders should be open to negotiations. Let's see how fair this one is."

Shelby laced her fingers together. "I don't even understand what any of it says."

He yanked a page out of the stack. "Like this for example. It says you have to pay a $125 fee and you agree to pay all office and legal fees before any work can start. By signing there, you're also agreeing that if you refuse to authorize additional changes that the contractor wants, then you will be billed an additional $750—per change. Then here—" Joel pulled another page out of the pile "—it says that if you file a complaint against them with the consumer office or the local police they are allowed to bill you $300."

Shelby's head started to spin with all the numbers. She pressed her temples. "How is that legal?"

"If you sign it, then you're saying you're okay with everything, so that makes it legal."

Shelby held up her hands. "Now I'm afraid to sign anything."

"Didn't you already sign something promising to work with this chump?" Joel used his thumb to point at Pekin over his shoulder.

She nodded.

"Then we're stuck working with him because I'm sure that contract reads a lot like this one where you'll be penalized if you decide to renege."

"Have I messed everything up?" She blinked against tears. Maybe she wasn't capable of handling things by herself. What if Caleb had been right to coddle her all along?

"No. We'll just keep a good eye on him." Joel softened his voice. "But promise me you'll stop paying him up front for things, okay? Paying ahead of time gives you less leverage to negotiate. We're going to make him change the contract to include progress payments that are directly linked to completed work. That'll ensure his men do the work in a timely manner, and he can't add additional charges later, because they'll be concerned with getting the agreed-upon amount."

She held his gaze. "Thank you for being here."

He let out a long breath and ran his hand through his hair. "I told you I'd come if you needed me."

"People sometimes say things like that just to be nice."

He stepped out of her reach. "When I say something, I mean it."

She touched his hand, but just for a second. "You might be the best person I know."

"I can assure you I'm not." He scooped up the papers and pushed them into her hands. "Do you want to talk to him, or should I?"

"I think it'll be best if you do all the talking."

"Okay, but I know you said you don't want a man taking over everything for you and overprotecting like Caleb does." He leaned closer. "I don't ever want you to feel like I'm doing that to you."

"You're not like Caleb at all. I asked for your help. Being like Caleb would have been barreling into this guy's office a week ago without my knowledge. Or something like that."

He laughed. "Is it all right, then, if I tell the contractor to make me the point person?" Joel locked the back of the SUV. "You're still in charge and will call all the shots. I'm just afraid if I don't say that, then he'll try to pressure you when I'm not around."

"That's fine. I trust you."

"Let's do this, then."

Shelby tucked the pages under one arm, then, feeling bold, grabbed hold of Joel's hand with her free one. His palm was calloused and work-worn. So was Joel— rough around the edges, but strong, steady and comforting. She wouldn't have had it any other way.

Joel cleared his throat to get Pekin's attention.

The man finished his phone conversation with a few curse words and then turned toward them. Within minutes of Joel laying out the changes he wanted to the contract, Pekin bristled visibly. The man loomed over Joel. He was twice as wide, but Joel didn't seem intimidated at all.

Joel pointed to the lot. "For the foundation, will you be using concrete block or poured concrete to full height?"

Pekin glared at Joel. "She signed in the first contract for the block."

"Fine. We'll have to work with that, then." Joel moved his jaw back and forth for a minute. "What do you fill the block with?"

"We don't. But the mortar we use—"

"You and I both know that concrete block is hollow and will cause the church's foundation to shift and crumble within a few years. They'll spend thousands of dollars fixing the foundation again and again. Mortar isn't going to stop that, so here are your choices." He ticked them off using two of his fingers. "You can change the contract at no charge since the work hasn't started yet to specify poured-in-place concrete, or you're going to reinforce the blocks with horizontal welded-wire and use vertical steel rods to reinforce them. Then you'll fill the voids of the block with pea gravel and coarse sand in each row before applying mortar."

Wow! Shelby was glad to have Joel around. As she watched the conversation ping-pong between the two men, she wanted to cheer each time Joel got the upper hand. Even so, he looked tired. And although she needed his help, a sense of guilt washed over her for adding more stress to his day. The second he finished talking to Pekin, she'd ask what had caused the bags under his eyes in the past forty-eight hours.

Joel shook hands with the contractor and the man stormed to his truck, slammed the door and drove off. Oh, well. As long as Pekin was going to make the changes to the contract and stop trying to pull one over on Shelby, he could throw as many fits as he wanted. Either way, it looked as though Joel would need to stop by the church building more often than he'd planned. He'd also put in a call to the city building department and let one of the inspectors know to keep a close eye on the church rebuild, as well.

With him, a city employee, and more than likely Caleb stopping by the site constantly, Pekin wouldn't try any more stunts. Joel felt bad that doing that would probably cost Miles another chance at arresting the low-life, but Joel wasn't okay letting Shelby's dream project serve as a testing ground, either. Miles could wait for the next person Pekin tried to con. It wasn't Joel's job to help the cop anyway.

Since Friday night she'd been sending him mixed signals. Sharing her dreams one second and avoiding contact with him the next. Joel couldn't stand mind games and wasn't going to put up with the yo-yo treatment for long.

She grabbed his hand and tugged him back across the street to his work truck. He leaned his back against the side of the vehicle and Shelby stopped. Six or so inches separated them. They were much closer than normal friends stood. Her cheeks were flushed, probably from being in jeans and long sleeves again on a ninety-degree day.

"You were great back there. A real hero."

Hero? Hardly. A hero would have been able to save the people on his calls last night.

Joel wiped his brow. As much as he cared about Shelby and enjoyed her company, right now he wanted to return to the station and zone out. Forget the past twelve hours had ever happened.

"Arguing with a man who could make string cheese out of me with his bare hands probably categorizes me as stupid more than anything else."

She glanced at his face, then the ground, his face and then the sky.

The awkward tension worked against his already raw nerves. Well, he could make that disappear. "Sorry about kissing you the other night."

Her eyes locked with his. "I'm not sorry."

"Really? Because it sure felt like you were. You avoided me the entire time at the fund-raiser."

"I was…confused." She brought her hands in front of her. "I have so much…baggage. I'm afraid to bring it into a relationship. It's the kind of stuff that will always be there. I haven't been able to trust a man yet." She stared at her laced fingers.

"You do realize you're looking at the king of baggage, right?"

"But that's different."

Of course it was. Shelby probably hadn't experienced anything on par with burning a church to a crisp. Speaking of which, he needed to ask her about what Chief Wheeler had said to him at the fund-raiser. How would Shelby be the one most healed by the rebuild?

"Why does rebuilding the church mean so much to you? I've asked you before, but you haven't answered. Not really."

"I guess…maybe I'm trying to bring back the past."

Joel frowned. "I don't want to live in the past. If we're going to be together I need you to understand that I'm focused on the future. I'd like to leave the past where it is."

"But the future is scary and uncertain. I don't even know what I'm going to do for a job tomorrow." She grimaced, but then he could tell she'd gotten an idea because her lips broke into a smile. "What about focusing on today only?"

"Today hasn't been so great. But I get what you're saying—live in the present—and I can do that."

She rested her hand on his forearm. "What happened?"

"Just a rough shift." Where he had failed people who

had counted on him. If he couldn't do a job he was trained for, why did he think he was capable of succeeding at something he knew nothing about—like a relationship? Shelby deserved better than him. Much better.

"Tell me. Please?" Her voice was so quiet he had to duck down to hear what she said.

Might as well break her bubble and tell her how un-hero-like he was.

"Can this count as my something personal to tell you today?" He'd promised to tell her one thing a day, but that hadn't happened after she avoided him on Saturday.

"Of course."

"We had two callouts. I couldn't save either person." He closed his eyes and instantly saw them—the beautiful teen girl who decided taking a handful of pills was better than facing her bullies, and then a middle-aged man with heart failure. The hopeless looks in the eyes of the man's wife and school-aged children when Joel told them the man was gone still stung like a road rash.

"I'm so sorry." She squeezed his arm.

"As an EMT, I'm not a stranger to death, but the people last night were…different. I can't explain it." He shoved his hands deep into his pants pockets. "It made me think about my own life. What am I doing all this for? You know? I've poured so much into my career because I had no one and nothing else, but if I die, then what? Besides Dante, no one would miss me, and I've done that by pulling away from anyone who's ever tried to care. I started thinking what would happen to me if I was injured and couldn't do my job. What would my life matter then? And it wouldn't."

"Your life matters, Joel. It matters to me."

How could she say that? They hardly knew each

other. Although, she probably knew him better than anyone presently.

He shook his head. "It doesn't. Not beyond my job." He splayed his hand over his chest. "And I've made it that way."

"That was the past, so let's not focus on that." She placed her hand over his. "We'll move forward. Together. Remember?"

If only it was that easy.

"Okay." The department radio in his work truck beeped. Someone at the station was looking for him. "I have to go."

She smiled up at him. "Real quick—would you be my date to Caleb's wedding on Saturday? Caleb told me he invited you."

For the first time that day, he was able to offer a genuine smile. "Sure, Shelby. I wouldn't miss it for the world."

Chapter Twelve

"You're stunning." Shelby straightened Paige's veil.

With beautiful styled waves in her blond hair and a fitted wedding dress that puffed out at the bottom, Paige looked like she'd walked right off the cover of a bridal magazine.

"So are you." Paige wrapped her arm around Shelby's shoulders. "Green's a good color on you."

Standing next to Paige and seeing their reflections in the wide mirror together should have made Shelby happy, but she couldn't help comparing herself to her almost sister-in-law and finding that she came up short. While Paige's smile was straight and white, Shelby had a crooked bottom tooth. Paige's hair and skin shimmered with a healthy glow and Shelby's makeup lacked any pop. Caleb often told Shelby he couldn't tell the difference when she did and didn't wear makeup—which he meant as a compliment, but it felt more like him saying she didn't know how to put on the stuff. It looked as though he was right.

Her mom never had taught Shelby any of the womanly secrets to beauty. They hadn't sat down in front of the mirror for a teaching session. She hadn't been shown different ways to enhance her eyes or cheekbones or how to cover up the freckles that pranced across her nose. And Mom hadn't shown her how to style her hair. For the past twenty years—or practically her whole life—Shelby's hairstyle had been the same. Too afraid of what people in Goose Harbor would think if she made a drastic change, she'd stayed the same. She hadn't rocked the boat and had tried to be someone who didn't cause any issues or need extra attention.

In doing so, she'd become someone who was easy to overlook and forget.

Shelby ran her hands up and down her arms and felt the patches of fire-damaged skin.

It all made sense. Mom hadn't seen her as beautiful. Because Shelby hadn't been and never would be. Not with the burns, and Mom had known that. She would have been wasting her time to show Shelby makeup and hair techniques.

Shelby yanked the matching blazer for her dress off the back of the chair where she'd placed it earlier. So far this morning, only Paige and Maggie had been getting ready in the nursery-turned-bride's room in the church where the wedding ceremony was to be held. Both of them had seen Shelby's scars before, so they didn't stare or ask questions. It had been nice to walk around all morning without wearing the constricting blazer. Now, with less than forty minutes until the wedding march, Shelby needed the security that came with covering up. No doubt the photographer would pop in at any moment and snap a few candid shots.

Her sudden dark mood didn't match the bright colors on the walls where murals depicted scenes from the

Bible. Or the knee-high chairs in every color of the rainbow grouped around each of the four small tables in the room. Shelby stared at the toy bins that lined the wall opposite the door and the row of cribs situated away from the windows. Not including the rehearsal the night before, she'd never been to this church before. Caleb and Paige had chosen the church because it had a huge lot that backed up to a forest preserve. Paige wanted an outdoor wedding and they'd picked a great location.

"Are you okay?" Paige had quietly taken up residence by her side again.

"Me?" Shelby startled. "Of course."

Her future sister-in-law gently turned Shelby so she could look her in the eyes. "It means a lot to me to have you standing up beside me, and even more that we're going to be sisters."

"Aren't you nervous for today? You're sounding so levelheaded." Shelby winked at her. "Shouldn't you be having a last-minute freak-out? I think that's standard issue for a bride right about now."

Paige shook her head. "No worries here. Caleb is... well, to me, Caleb is home." She shrugged. "That probably makes no sense whatsoever, but I can't think of a better way to say it."

In a room nearby, the cellist and singer began to practice the song they would perform while Caleb and Paige prayed with the pastor during the ceremony. The cello's deep, soulful notes filled the room.

The performer started to sing. "'I will always stay beside you. We'll celebrate the best of times and hold each other during all of life's storms.'"

The singer's rich voice mixed with the cello in perfect harmony. Shelby swallowed hard as the words worked their way to her heart. Who would hold her when life's storms hit? She wanted someone beside her—more than ever. For the first time in a long time, she wanted to be noticed. Was it so bad to desire attention and love?

But she'd have to ponder relationships and her future another day, because today the focus needed to stay on Paige and Caleb. They couldn't spend time feeling bad for her when they were supposed to be celebrating.

She offered Paige a big smile. "I probably haven't told you enough, but I'm glad you came into my brother's life when you did. Caleb was really messed up for a while after Sarah's death."

"Oh, when we met, I was just as lost as he was."

"True. But you were fresh off a breakup. It's not like you had any time to process or heal."

"Honestly, it doesn't matter if it had been a day or two years since I'd experienced the pain. In this life we're all fresh off some hurt or let down. The fact is, everyone carries around baggage. Every single one of us. But once you find someone who loves you with the scars, just hang on to them, okay?"

Scars. Did she have to use that word?

Shelby fixed her vision on a cartoon hippo painted on the wall near a depiction of baby Moses in a basket. "What if the person doesn't know about the scars?" she whispered.

Paige took her hand. "Then it might be about time to decide if the man is worth trusting. If so, then tell him, and after that, when you work up the courage, show him."

"Not today." Shelby released Paige's hand. "I couldn't. Not with everyone here. I'm wearing this blazer." She grabbed the bottom of the garment for emphasis.

"Of course not today." Paige snagged Shelby's arm, stopping her from fidgeting. "No one wants to make you uncomfortable. But someday you'll have to tell someone about your secret, and the longer you put it off, the harder it will be to explain why you didn't believe he should know. That or he's going to wonder if you question his character."

Shelby bit her bottom lip. As usual, Paige was right—especially when it came to Joel. "And given Joel's background with all the foster care problems, he probably already has trust issues. So learning I kept something so big from him could upset him."

"I don't know Joel at all, but I wonder if he'll be honored that you'd trust him with such personal information." She paused and her eyes lit up. "Yes, I think he'll react by—"

A knock sounded on the door and Maggie popped her head inside. "Are you girls ready?"

"Is it time?" Paige grinned.

Joel would react how? Shelby's stomach dropped. If it hadn't been Paige's wedding day, she would have brought the conversation back to her and Joel, but they'd spent enough time talking about Shelby's problems today. The conversation had to be left where it was. Today was Paige's day, after all.

"Almost." Maggie squeezed in through the almost-closed door before shutting it quickly. She'd been darting in and out all day and hadn't wanted to open the door all the way in case someone saw Paige before the wedding started. "It's time to pray, then the photographer will come in and then it's showtime, ladies."

"I can't wait." Shelby laughed.

"Me, too." Paige nudged Shelby. "This will go down in history as one of my favorite days ever."

As Maggie motioned for them to take seats around a kid-sized table, Shelby couldn't help but silently agree with Paige. This would be a great day. And some of the pleasure for her came from the fact that Caleb had wrangled Joel into walking with Shelby down the aisle and standing up as his second groomsman.

Truth be known, Joel's usual mode of operation included skipping wedding celebrations. Who needed a reminder that many people grew up and enjoyed happy, functional lives?

Not him.

Yet he'd shown up for Caleb's big day, and not just that, he'd let himself get talked into being a last-minute groomsman. Thankfully, they'd kept the ceremony portion short. Joel hadn't picked the best shoes to wear, and standing any longer would have caused blisters to form. He'd bought the dress shoes years ago and couldn't remember ever wearing them. The uneven ground had been hard to stand on comfortably, too, although Shelby and Maggie probably had the harder time of it in their heels. At one point he'd caught Shelby's eye and she'd mouthed *I'm sinking!* Sure enough, her high dress shoes had been stuck an inch deep in the ground when they'd tried to walk back down the aisle.

As he made his way around the back of the church, the words from the song sung during the ceremony ran through his mind.

I will always stay beside you.

No other human being had ever said that to Joel, but

then, had he ever been willing to speak those words to another person? No. Why hadn't it occurred to him to flip the question around like that before? For so long, he'd been focused on the perceived wrongs done to him. If he was being honest, he'd been beyond angry with humanity in general for deciding he wasn't worth anyone's time. Without realizing it, he'd lived his life in a way that said he didn't care about the rest of the world, either. Keeping people at arm's length. Downright avoiding friendships and finding reasons to break off the few connections he had made.

Joel spoke a good game of wanting roots and friends, but chose again and again not to foster that lifestyle at all.

He fisted his hands. How foolish. He'd lived such a shallow existence, and it had to change. It would change. Starting now.

He spotted Shelby near the opening of the white tent where the reception would be held and waved. A huge smile spread across her face, and she motioned for him to join her as she greeted the crowd and handed each person their seating card.

Life up until now might have been only half-lived, but in Goose Harbor, he'd change that. Hopefully, his new life would include Shelby. Not just because it would be rough starting all over again with someone else, but he didn't want anyone else. Shelby's kind and generous spirit made him want to always be around her. She made him imagine life in a new way—in a way that included a woman beside him.

Joel ran his hand over the top of his hair and started to make his way to Shelby. Halfway there, he saw Caleb and held out a hand to congratulate him for the twentieth time today.

"I'm really happy for you, man. You're so blessed to have found the one woman you were meant to be with." He was talking to Caleb, but his eyes found Shelby.

Caleb snagged his arm and pulled him toward the church building. "Do you have a second to talk?"

Had he said something wrong? "It's your wedding. Do *you* have a second?"

"Sure." Caleb laughed and held the back door open for him. "It's not like they'll start anything until Paige and I go to the tent. Anyway, she wanted a moment alone to talk with her parents."

They walked down the hallway to a large classroom with a bunch of couches in it. No doubt a high school group met here. Caleb plopped down and let out a deep breath.

Tension flooded Joel's back and shoulders as he perched on the armrest. "What did you want to talk about?"

"Don't look so worried."

"I have a feeling this can't be good." Could Caleb have changed his mind since basically giving his blessing last weekend?

His old friend leaned forward and pressed the tips of his fingers together. "You said I found the one woman I was meant to be with, but you're wrong. Paige isn't the only woman for me."

Joel's head spun. "What are you talking about? If you had doubts you should have dealt with them before the ceremony."

Caleb held up his hand. "Not like that. I love Paige. She's my life. I have no doubts about our life together.

Whatsoever. But I have a gut feeling that I need to tell you about Sarah."

"Sarah West? She's the girl you were dating when I left, right?"

Caleb nodded.

"You two used to talk about getting married." Joel eased back into the couch. If Caleb wanted to talk old loves, he could be here for him. "I thought about that after I saw you the first day at the firehouse. Some childhood dreams don't come true, but it looks like it all worked out for you."

"But that's the thing, I did marry Sarah."

Joel crossed his arms over his chest. "Now I'm confused."

"I got my childhood dream. Sarah and I married and had a few great years together. Blessed years." He stared up at the ceiling. "She was shot outside the mentoring center she founded in Brookside."

What could Joel say? It was a tragedy. He stared at Caleb. Even back in the day, Brookside had been an urban nightmare full of gangs and random violence. If they'd wanted a thrill, teens in Goose Harbor used to challenge each other to drive to Brookside and cruise the main street with their doors unlocked. He could only imagine how dangerous it had become after the economic downturn.

But shot? "I'm so sorry." His words came out so much softer than they'd sounded in his head.

"Thank you. It was hard. Who am I kidding? It's still hard." Caleb stood and paced a few feet away.

Joel inched to the edge of the couch. "Why are you telling me this?"

Caleb faced him. "Because childhood dreams can

come true—all dreams can. But dreams, both getting them and living them, aren't always easy and pain free."

"Okay." Why was he saying all of these things?

"Back when we were teens, you dreamed of a family. I want you to know you can stop looking. You have that here."

"But I—"

"Families don't always look like what we think they will. Take me. I no longer have parents, but I have Shelby, and Maggie might be my first wife's sister, but she's become like family to me. Now I have Paige. I misjudged you at first, but if you're willing to forgive me, you're welcome to be part of our patchwork family. If you want to be."

Tears stung the back of Joel's eyes. "I forgave you when you asked. That's done."

"Good." Caleb smiled. "But don't remember the pain part, okay? Sometimes dreams look different when we live them, but they're still good and God's still in control of them. Just hang on to that."

"I will. Thank you. I don't know what else to say."

"You don't need to say anything else. But time's a wasting, brother. Let's go celebrate." Caleb held out his hand and helped Joel off the couch.

As Joel walked back outside with Caleb, a million thoughts ran through his head. The loudest one, though, was a single word: *family*. A lifetime of wishing for that conversation and it had happened. Sure, it wasn't like he'd pictured all those years ago. Not a couple of parents asking if he wanted them to adopt him, but God was his parent, right? And now he could add sibling-like friendships.

Caleb was right. Dreams could come true.

Chapter Thirteen

Shelby glanced over at Joel as he parked his truck in the lot near the beach. After spending most of the reception flirting with each other, they'd decided to head back to Goose Harbor for a midnight stroll. They'd stopped at her apartment so she could change into sweats and walking shoes. He'd brought a change of clothes to the wedding and had changed out of his suit at the church, but they'd still swung by his place to pick up Dante so he could join in the fun.

Joel pulled out a pack of cinnamon gum and offered her a piece.

She shook her head. "You're always chewing that stuff."

He tossed the pack of gum onto the dashboard. "That's because a teen at one of my foster homes told me that Frankenstein came after boys that smelled like mint."

"That's horrible!" She hid a laugh.

Joel winked at her. "I was terrified and haven't used mint-flavored anything since. Cinnamon gum and toothpaste became my standby."

"So you're still afraid of Frankenstein?"

"I'll never tell. Besides, this story was your personal thing from me for the day. You'll have to ask about Frankenstein tomorrow."

"I just might." She stretched her toes. "It feels amazing being out of those heels."

"I'll take your word for it." Joel grinned at her and her heart squeezed. He really was such a handsome man. With his black hair, deep hazel eyes and a dark five-o'clock shadow across his jaw, he possessed many of the qualities that lent themselves to a bad-boy vibe, but his character was far from the look. She doubted he'd ever intentionally hurt anyone or anything. After all, one of the main duties of his job was saving lives.

It was interesting how things worked out in life. Take Joel's profession, for example. Ever since the fire, Shelby had secretly admired firefighters. A man in a face mask and fire suit had been her hero that day. So, of course, she would like firefighters above all others. Now she sat beside one, and more than likely he would be the first man she trusted with her guarded secret.

Dante wiggled with excitement when Joel opened his truck door.

Joel wrapped the leash twice around his hand. "He might be old and arthritic, but he can still be a handful, especially when he catches wind of something."

"I know!" She swung out of her side of the vehicle. An image of the last time she'd walked Dante flashed through her mind. She had been texting Maggie on her phone while the dog had plodded along, and before she had known what was happening, Dante had taken off. "Sometimes when he sees a squirrel I feel like he's going to take my arm out of its socket. It's a good thing he listens well."

Shelby set a slow pace down the beach that Joel matched.

"When he can hear you. Poor old guy."

Encouraged by Joel's warm smile and still feeling sentimental from the wedding, Shelby situated herself by Joel's side and took hold of his hand. He repositioned it so their fingers could lace together.

Their shoes squeaked in the sand. A fish flipped out of the water a couple of feet offshore. Dante barked and jolted for the water, making them both laugh.

Shelby broke the silence first. "Speaking of walking dogs, I got a lead on a possible new client today."

"Tell me about it."

"I was talking to Jenna Crest at the wedding and she said her neighbors were looking for someone to walk their golden retriever while they were at work. It sounds like he's young and has a lot of energy. He's been chewing their furniture while they're both at work." A gust of wind tossed cold air from the lake at them. Shelby shivered and tugged up the hood of her sweatshirt. "They live on the edge of town so I can bike there until the weather gets bad and, hopefully by then, I'll have a car."

Joel pumped her hand once. "That sounds like a start. I've been wondering if you've given any more thought to what you wanted to do going forward."

"With us?"

He coughed in a failed attempt to hide a chuckle. "I thought that was pretty evident."

"Oh. Right." Heat rose up her neck. Thankfully, it was too dark outside for him to be able to see it, and even if it hadn't been, her hood would have covered her embarrassment. "You meant about working."

"If I'm remembering correctly, you said you wanted to figure out something where you wouldn't have to travel from home to home, but you could still work with dogs."

She shrugged. "As you can see, I'm no closer to coming up with an idea than I was all those weeks ago. I don't have a college degree to flash around at businesses to secure a job, and I can't imagine sitting behind a desk for the rest of my life anyway." If only she'd been brave enough to do what she had wanted all those years ago. Venture out. But it was too late now. "I'm left with few options. If the money situation gets really bad, I can probably get a summer job at the candy shop or one of the restaurants in town, but that would be temporary at best. Looks like I'm stuck dog-sitting."

"What about being a dog obedience instructor? You have such a talent for calming animals. It'd be a shame to waste a gift like that."

Shelby stopped and studied Joel's face, and found his expression open and sincere. He wasn't teasing her. He saw value in pursuing a vocation she loved. Everyone else told her she'd grow out of her love for dogs one day. That she'd need a *real job* at some point. Not Joel. He suggested options she hadn't thought about. He encouraged her passion when others didn't even try to understand it.

She toed the sand. "I think you have to have a certificate to prove you know what you're doing."

"Well, we'll think of something." He crossed his arms and looked out over the lake. "Okay, I've got it.

Rent out a storefront and set up a doggy day care facility."

She grinned. "That idea actually has some promise."

He tapped his forehead and then took her hand again. "I get a good one every couple of years."

She bumped her shoulder into his. "Don't sell yourself short. I'd say you at least have to have one good one a year."

"We'll go with that estimate, then." Giving her hand a light tug, he brought her to an abrupt stop so he could turn her gently to face him. "But seriously, Shelby, I believe in you and I think you're capable of chasing after whatever your heart desires."

Like a drummer at a rock concert, her heart pounded a crazy rhythm. She rested her hands on his chest. "Anything?" she whispered.

The corners of Joel's mouth crinkled into a warm smile. "Your brother reminded me today that dreams are worth pursuing. I think he's right."

Shelby playfully pushed on his chest. "My brother said that? Now I know you're making this up."

"He did. Honest."

"Hmm." She squinted at him, but hoped her slight smile let him know she was joking. "How do I know you're not making this up to tease me?"

Joel looked away for a moment, then locked eyes with her. "Don't you trust me?" His voice was quiet and held a serious tone.

"Yes," she whispered. "I trust you." The muscles in her shoulders relaxed just from saying the words. She'd chosen to trust Joel. Should she tell him about the fire? Finally explain why the church's rebuild meant so much to her? Share how he'd already made an impact on her life?

A steady swoosh of water moving behind her became the only sound in her head. Now was her moment to open up.

Joel grinned. "Good. Then believe me, even Caleb can have a good idea once in a while." He winked.

Shelby felt pressure at the back of her knees and suddenly she was shoved against Joel. With a thud, they toppled to the sand.

"Sorry. Sorry." Joel recovered before she did. He rolled to his side and sat up, kicking his legs a bit in the process. She rubbed her forehead. She'd banged it against Joel's shoulder as they fell. "What—"

Joel chuckled. "Dante must have walked a couple of circles around us as we were talking." He unwound the leash from around their knees. "I should have been paying better attention."

Shelby stood and shook sand from her shirt and pants. In the process, one of her sleeves rode up her wrist by a few inches. She froze. The moon was out, but it was still too dark for him to notice the raised skin on her arm. Still, a sense of empowerment surged through her veins when she decided not to push the sleeve down right away. She helped him stand and they both teased Dante about playing a trick on them.

The special moment where she could have been honest had passed. They were back to kidding and tossing branches in the water to entertain the dog. It would ruin the night now to begin such a serious discussion.

When they returned to the truck, Shelby instinctively pushed down her sleeve. But she would tell him one day. Soon. She'd do it.

But not tonight.

* * *

No matter how many years he'd been an EMT, there probably would never come a day when Joel felt mentally ready to face a 9-1-1 call. Sure, he knew what to do and he could go through the motions for any emergency situation, almost as if his hands took over and performed whatever tasks needed to be done, all the while trying to keep his emotions at bay.

People who worked as first responders needed to function that way. Either that or they would be emotionally spent from allowing their compassion and desire to connect with their patients to get in the way. *Do the job and leave.* That had been Joel's motto, but should that be his mode of operation now that he'd decided to put down roots into Goose Harbor's sandy soil?

Whenever Chief Wheeler joined the team on a call, he would hug the family members involved, ask about prior problems he was familiar with, and often pray with the hurting person if they were open to that sort of thing. Wheeler was beloved in Goose Harbor because he practiced compassion and connected directly with the people he served. Joel could take a lesson from him, but he needed to find a way to ask Wheeler how he did it and stayed sane.

The ambulance stopped and Joel hurtled out the passenger side. He got to the porch steps first.

An older woman held open the front door. "Hurry. She's bleeding pretty good. We have her at the kitchen table."

"What's the injury from?" He rushed into the house and his vision swept the area in a mechanical way, searching for the necessary clues to a dangerous situation.

"Dog bite, I'm afraid." A man held a barking gold dog by a choke collar. A retriever.

A wave of nausea washed through his stomach. *Shelby*. Rounding the man and the dog, he doubled his speed and burst into the kitchen.

Shelby sat at the table holding a towel around her forearm. "Joel." How deep was the bite? How long had they delayed the call? Was she in a lot of pain?

He pulled out the chair next to her and commanded his voice to stay calm. "On a scale of one to ten, how much pain are you in?"

"I'm fine." She hugged her arm to her stomach.

"Here, let me take a look at it." He reached for the towel.

Shelby jolted back and stood, knocking over her chair. "No. I don't need that."

Shock? That had to be it. Nothing else explained her reaction.

He rose slowly. "You're going to be okay. I'm here to help you, but I can't until I have a look at your arm. We also need to get you into the ambulance."

Tears started to drip off her chin. She wouldn't make eye contact with him. "I don't want your help."

Why was Shelby acting like this? *Practice compassion*. But he was, and it didn't seem to matter.

The rest of the crew had entered the room but hadn't spoken, and their presence made the air in the room heavy.

"Shelby, come on. Don't you trust me?" Why had he tossed that out there in front of everyone? She'd said she did last night. But then why refuse his help today?

She cradled her arm. "Not in this."

Her words stung with the force of a backhand to the

jaw. Worse. If she didn't trust him in the one aspect of his life where he was completely competent, then she couldn't trust him in all the relationship ways he was bound to bungle.

He breathed deep and worked his jaw back and forth. His voice took on a hard edge. "I'm sure you realize that dog bites can lead to serious infection. Especially untreated bites. Staphylococcus and streptococcus being a couple of the worst, but local infections can be just as bad. Even if you don't get an infection, the damage to muscle, tendons, blood vessels and nerves can be irreversible if there is too much time before treatment. Sometimes surgery can't even repair the mark."

As he spoke, Shelby narrowed her eyes. She turned her body so her injured arm was blocked from his view. "And making sure everything looks nice is all that matters, right? That whatever marks the dog left goes away without any scars."

"You're being ridiculous." And he was being unprofessional, but he couldn't find the internal switch he usually used to turn off his emotions. He'd been wrong about Shelby. She couldn't care about him like he'd let himself care for her. Not if she couldn't let him take care of her in the one way he knew how. "So you're refusing treatment?"

"I am." Her voice shook.

"Then sign this." He yanked the refusal form out of his duty bag and slammed it on the table. "Give it to one of the guys." Joel spun around and started to push through the rest of his team to get out of the house.

"Joel…please." The hurt in her voice stopped him, but he didn't turn around.

"Since you can't trust us, you should probably go

find someone you can and get them to treat the bite. You think I'm overreacting, but they can be serious."

Not waiting for an answer, Joel pounded down the front steps and punched the side of the ambulance before barreling inside the vehicle.

On the drive back to the fire department he turned the radio to a blaring level so the other men couldn't say anything to him. Besides, he had to drown out the words playing through his head like a looping video.

You'll never be good enough. No one wants you.

Caleb was wrong. Dreams weren't worth the pain. Opening himself up to the idea of a relationship with Shelby had been a mistake. One he hoped not to make again.

Chapter Fourteen

When she'd asked at the appointment, Doctor Brandon said she could go into Lake Michigan thirty-six hours after getting the stitches, as long as she promised not to do any marathon swimming, and to contact him if she noticed any redness or swelling near the bite area. It helped to have a doctor in town who knew about her skin and kept her secret.

Thankfully, he told her that yes, the bite had bled a lot, but it wasn't deep enough to cause lasting complications. The dog's sharper teeth had landed around her scars and since that skin was thicker, its teeth hadn't penetrated as badly as they would have otherwise.

She folded her sweatpants and put them beside her shirt and towel at the sandy base of the dock. The water was chilled from the night, plus Lake Michigan never really got warm until late August. No matter. An early-morning swim would help clear her mind like it always did. And she had a lot on her mind.

Joel hadn't called or returned any messages in the past three days. Why should he? She'd made him look foolish in front of his coworkers, had shoved him away in front of everyone. That aspect of the situation bothered her the most. Joel probably felt abandoned again, and he may not want to talk to her.

She couldn't blame him. Maybe it was easier this way because his panicked reaction to the possibility of a lasting mark from the bite meant they couldn't have a relationship. Not now or ever. Staying friends would only make it hurt more. While her mind understood that ending their relationship early was for the best—because it minimized how great the pain would have been when he eventually rejected her—her heart still protested.

Her relationship with Joel was supposed to be different. She'd thought he'd be the one who could love her as she was. But maybe no one could.

"Let go of it, Shelby. Just let go."

She walked deeper into the water until it lapped against her chin. Pumping her arms and legs, a sense of freedom surged through her veins. On her morning swims, she could be herself. Skin and scars exposed, with no need to hide and cover up in shame. If only the rest of the world would accept her the way the morning air did.

She paddled farther out than usual, out past the end of the long pier into deeper waters, determined to get away from Goose Harbor for ten minutes and forget the past couple of days. With Paige and Caleb gone on their honeymoon and Maggie busy with her inn during tourist season, she had no one to talk to.

Rolling onto her back, she put out her hands and floated. Eyes focused on the deep gray sky, she decided to talk to God out loud.

"I don't have to hide from You, either, do I? You

know I look like this. You used those firefighters to save me from the church all those years ago, so You must have wanted me to live my life like this. Well, that makes me angry. There. I said it."

She breathed deeply and swam back to the end of the pier. It was the longest pier in the state's coast of Lake Michigan.

"But I know these scars mean nothing to You. You still see me the same as always, don't You? And love me. Just as I am." She ran her hands over the slimy baseboards and kicked her legs. "Thank You for that. I hope I'm not asking too much, but is it possible that someone else could love me. A person? A man? I still dream of being a wife and a mom. Should I give those dreams up?"

The pier creaked. "Shelby?"

She squeezed her eyes closed. Joel. Why was he out here now during her sacred alone time? How much of her prayer had he overheard?

Keeping everything below water except for her head, she let go of the pier and paddled into the open water before turning around. For once, she found herself thankful that the lake's water was murky instead of the clear water she'd seen in ads for Caribbean beaches. This far out into the water, Lake Michigan was a friend who could hide her, as long as she could convince Joel to leave.

Even so, her energy wouldn't last much longer and she'd have to come out of the water sooner than later.

"What are you doing here?" Shelby hollered from thirty feet away.

Joel opened his mouth to answer her, but stopped when he heard the sky rumble. While he'd walked the beach, dark clouds had rolled in to blanket the earth. They were the type of clouds that piled up like people waiting in line for a midnight showing of the latest overproduced teen movie—angry and ready to rain down fury at a moment's notice. These were the type of summer storm clouds that held house-shaking thunder, Olympic-sized pools worth of rain, and dent-causing hail.

Shelby needed to get out of the water.

He cupped his hands around his mouth. "You better come in. It's going to storm."

"You didn't answer my question." She spoke loudly, but her voice and breathing sounded labored. A storm and a weary swimmer made the worst possible scenario he could think of at the moment.

After a night tossing and turning, he didn't feel up to arguing with her. He just wanted her safe. For the past few days, he'd been watching the news footage about a wildfire raging in Colorado. A lot of people were in danger and a thought kept tugging at the back of his mind to go and offer his help and training. He might not be a member of a hotshot crew anymore, but his certifications were all up-to-date. He might be of some good to someone out there. Unlike here where his semigirlfriend wouldn't even let him treat a simple dog bite.

"Oddly enough, I came to the beach to think about you." Joel slipped off his gym shoes. Being off duty, he didn't have to follow protocol and listen if she said she didn't need his help. He'd jump in and drag her out of the water if he had to.

"About me?" She coughed. "We need to talk."

"Not now. You're tired, Shelb. You've got to get out of the water."

The first bolt of lightning ripped across the sky.

Shelby's eyes widened, but she stayed where she was. "I'll get out when you leave."

First refusing his help with the dog bite and now not taking him seriously about the danger of swimming during a storm. What reason could she possibly have for acting this way? She had said she dressed in long sleeves and pants because of modesty. But she must know he'd seen a woman in a swimsuit before and, given the circumstances, it wasn't like he'd have time to check her out, if that was her main worry.

At the risk of embarrassing her, he called out again, "Now's not the time for modesty."

"It's not about that."

Okay. No more trying to understand her reasons. He yanked off his sweatshirt.

She swam a little closer. "What are you doing?"

"Getting ready to jump in there after you."

"Don't." She palmed her cheek to wipe away tears. The action made her dip a bit farther beneath the water. "Please don't."

"Then come out."

"Please. Leave. I'll come out then."

He shook his head. "After the dog bite, I'm not certain you will. So I'm going to wait right here until I see you out and safe."

Lightning cracked across the sky.

It looked as if he was going for a swim. Joel yanked off his shoes. "Soon would be good."

"Could you go back to the beach and turn around? I'll come out as long as you turn your back to me."

Her voice trembled. A mixture of cold, exhaustion and terror.

Whatever it took. He turned around, picked up his sweatshirt and shoes, and slowly made his way toward the beach. The pier groaned behind him, signaling that Shelby had hoisted herself out of the water.

Joel stopped a few feet away from her pile of clothes on the beach. "Walk quick, okay?"

The pier creaked with her footsteps and then he heard the soft pad of her feet when she transitioned to the sand. A light rain began to drum against the pier.

"Oh, no." She gasped.

He spun around to see what had happened.

Shelby had her back to him as she fished her shirt out of the water. Which was an exercise in futility seeing as the rain grew harder every second.

Joel rushed to grab her towel before the wind took it for a swim, as well. He froze. Across Shelby's back, down her legs, and on the backs of both arms were patches of angry skin. Large scars, the leftover of healed burns.

A man he had worked with in Indy had been caught in a fire and suffered third-degree burns from the ordeal. His skin had looked just like Shelby's.

The marks explained why she wore pants and long sleeves all the time. But why hide them? Had someone made fun of her? He balled up his fists. Didn't she know that all those marks meant was that she was strong and brave?

What now? He could turn back around and pretend he hadn't seen or he could tell her the scars were nothing to him, and she had no reason to hide where he was concerned.

Joel chose the latter. "Here." He held out his sweat-shirt. "Don't bother with that waterlogged shirt. You can wear this."

Shelby bolted up and let her drenched shirt fall onto the wet sand with a thud.

Don't cry. Don't break down. Not here. Not in front of him.

A tremor worked its way up Shelby's spine and she fought against her shaking hands. "You weren't sup-posed to turn around."

"Shelby." His voice was calm and gentle, probably a result of his fireman training. "Please look at me."

She obeyed, slowly. "I know you must think—"

He grabbed her hand and tugged her to jog beside him. "My truck's not far. Let's get there before the sky really breaks open."

The rain beat hard against her back. She shivered as he yanked open the passenger door and helped her climb inside.

"Put these on." He tossed her sweatpants and his sweatshirt into her lap before closing the door. Of course—he'd want her to cover her scars as soon as she could so he wouldn't have to look at them anymore.

As much as she would have liked to be dramatic and toss his sweatshirt in his face, she was shivering. She needed its warmth.

He climbed into the driver's seat and shoved the keys into the engine. "It'll take a second for the heat to kick in. Sorry."

Might as well get the talk over with. "I understand if you don't want to be around me anymore now that you know."

He leaned against the driver's door so he faced her. "Were you ever planning on telling me?"

Studying her puckered fingertips became the most important thing in the world. "I almost did after the wedding. I wanted to. I planned to."

"Why didn't you?" His voice was soft again, casual instead of accusatory as she'd imagined it would be.

She threw up her hands. "Because of *this*. Because now you'll treat me differently. You might not say it, but you find me repulsive. It's really hard getting rejected again and again."

"Has someone—has a guy—done that to you? Rejected you after he found out?" He was fighting hard to control the edge in his voice now—she could tell. Was he mad at her? Or mad at the idea of someone rejecting her?

"I never actually told any of them. But they would have."

Joel scooted closer and laid a hand on her arm. "Forgive my boldness, but it sounds like Shelby's the only one rejecting Shelby. Does that make sense? There's enough hurt in this world without doing that to yourself."

Something in his words rang true. She'd always hidden the scars. She'd been ashamed of how she looked. But had she even offered other people the chance to reject her? Or had she rejected herself and figured everyone else would do the same?

She leaned her head against the headrest and closed her eyes tightly. "You saw me."

He pushed up her sleeve. She started to yank her arm away, but he held fast. As he traced his thumb over the scar wrapping around her wrist, she knew he waited for her to open her eyes and look at him. When she did, he offered a tentative smile.

"One. I fight fires for a living. Seeing burns is part of the job and these scars aren't bad or ugly or whatever it is you're afraid of. Two. All these mean is that you have a story to tell. Besides that, to me, you're the same Shelby who kept me awake thinking about her all last night." He pushed up the sleeve on her other arm to reveal a second scar. "I care about you. These don't change who you are or my attraction to you."

She stared at his hands on her marks. He cupped her arms and ran his thumbs back and forth over the scars. How could he do that without gagging? "You're not grossed out?"

"Not at all."

"I'm having a hard time believing you."

His fingers stopped moving when he grazed where her stitches were. "Your scars—is that why you wouldn't let me treat your dog bite the other day?"

She swallowed hard and nodded. "There were so many people there, and I didn't want you to find out like that."

"Well, I know now. So what do we do?"

"I guess that's up to you." She studied the way his fingers looked as they rested against her scars. "But if this changes things between us, I understand."

Joel locked gazes with her as he brought one of her arms to his lips and kissed the scar. He repeated it on the second arm. Then he brought his hands to cradle her head and he kissed her soundly on the mouth. She felt like she was drowning. As if she wouldn't be able to take another breath and it didn't matter or worry her.

Could he really care about her enough to look beyond her scars? Even better, could he love her—scars and all?

Chapter Fifteen

Joel turned the heat to full blast and then put the truck in Drive. "You've got to be cold. Let's get you home."

She buckled her seat belt and laughed. "After a kiss like that, I'm surprisingly warm."

The window wipers were flying at full speed as he pulled out of the parking lot. "You deserve to be cherished. Just as you are. Remember that. Okay?"

"I'll keep trying to believe that."

"Well, just so you know, I'm not going to stop telling you." He laid his right arm over the back of her seat.

"It might take a few more of those kisses."

He glanced at her and his face broke into an uncharacteristic grin. "I have plenty of those left to spare."

Unbuckling her seat belt, she scooted over into the middle seat and buckled up there. Her side was against his. She laid her head on his biceps. "Thanks for being so wonderful."

At the stop sign, he dropped a light kiss on top of her hair. "You're welcome...I think that's the right answer. Or was that a trick?"

"No tricks. No more hiding. Only the truth from now

on." She pulled his right arm so it curled around her and she could hold his hand. "I like being next to you."

"Me, too."

Now that he knew about Shelby's scars, they could move forward. He'd thought they were done—that *he* was done with all relationships—after the dog bite incident. But that situation made sense now. She hadn't been rejecting him or saying she didn't trust him. Well, maybe the trust part was partially true—but not in a bad way. More than anyone, he understood the paralyzing fear of being rejected and knew how much it could set the course of a person's life.

She sighed. "You've asked me a couple of times why the church rebuild is so important to me. It has to do with my burns. See, I was inside the church when it caught fire."

Joel's heart stuttered. When the church caught fire? But then that meant… The contents of his stomach were going to make a grand reappearance. He sucked air in through his mouth.

It couldn't be from the church in Goose Harbor. No one had been inside when he torched it. He'd looked in the windows and everything.

Unaware of his personal torment, Shelby continued with her story. "I went there to pray after finding out my dad was never going to come back. I knelt down with my head resting on the pew and asked God to give me the family I wanted. A strong husband who loved his wife no matter what, and children who were wanted and played with and cared for."

If she'd been kneeling in the pew, he *might not* have seen her. Correction, from his vantage point peering in the windows, he wouldn't have been able to see her in that position. No way. His careless fit of sixteen-year-old rage had hurt Shelby—not just God, as he'd intended. He had hurt her physically, mentally and emotionally. All from one selfish action.

Sweat broke out on his forehead and the palms of his hands. He unwound his arm from her and gripped the steering wheel with both hands. "The roads are slick."

What had he done?

Shelby nodded. "I didn't realize the church was burning and I got trapped in there. As I was trying to get out, a ceiling beam fell and pinned me. I passed out at some point and woke up in the arms of a fireman carrying me out. That might explain why I have a thing for firefighters, huh?" She squeezed his arm.

It must have been his imagination, but where she touched him felt seared with fire. *Tell her. Tell her the truth. Now. Do it.*

He could hardly see the road through the rain, so he leaned forward to squint through the windshield. The movement also served to untangle Shelby from his arm. As much as he cared for her, at the moment, he couldn't stomach her expressing her feelings for him or showing her love through physical contact. He'd ruined her life. Completely. She'd hate him when she found out. How could she not?

No more hiding. Only the truth from now on.

Her words, spoken only minutes ago, rushed back to taunt him.

But he couldn't tell her the truth. Not about the fire. What good would it serve for her to find out he had been the source of all her problems? None. He'd be rejected again, and she'd feel like he'd played some huge joke on her.

Besides, it wasn't about not telling the truth. There was a difference between lying and not offering information. Right? Sure, he'd been upset back at the beach to learn Shelby had kept something huge from him. But his situation was different. Much different.

He rammed his gear stick into Park in the closest spot outside her apartment. Shelby undid her seat belt and faced him. "I realized recently that I wrapped a lot of my healing up in the church being rebuilt. It was silly, but I felt like I couldn't move on until the church was standing again. I'm glad for all that now—don't you see? All that time, I thought I was missing out on life and on dating, but in reality, God was keeping me safe until I could be with you."

He studied the leather on the steering wheel. "Shelby...don't put everything on me, I—"

She framed his face with her hands and rested her forehead against his. "You have changed my life. Don't ever doubt that. I care about you so much, and I can't wait to see what God has in store for us." Offering one quick, sweet kiss, Shelby jumped out of the truck and darted for her apartment.

For the first time since he'd returned to Goose Harbor, Joel didn't wait until she was safely inside. The second the passenger door closed, he shoved the gear into Reverse and raced for the interstate. He needed to drive. For hours.

Like angry fists, the rain pounded against his truck. Every couple of minutes, lightning shattered across the sky, making it easier to see the lines on the road beneath the puddles pooling on the concrete.

His truck began to shake as he forced it past seventy miles an hour. Thoughts whizzed in his mind with the speed of a championship table tennis match. Each one contradicted the next. He had to tell her. He could never tell her. He had to tell her. Maybe he should leave Goose Harbor. *Stop running from problems.*

Swerving off at an exit, he followed the signs that guided him to a nature preserve. No other cars were in the lot, probably because of the storm. He cut the engine and threw himself back against the headrest with a deep breath.

You have changed my life.

"You're right there. But not in the way you imagined." Joel steepled his fingers and rested the tips against his nose as he closed his eyes. "God, what am I supposed to do? You led me back to Goose Harbor for this? It seems cruel. I know I made mistakes." Don't minimize issues. "I know I sinned against You. But I thought You said once forgiveness is given, You make the transgression go away. It sure doesn't feel like that. This one keeps coming back again and again. I'll never be anything but the man who set fire to that church. Will I?"

Shelby reached across the small table at Fair Tradewinds Coffee to squeeze Paige's tanned hand. "Tell me all about the honeymoon."

Paige couldn't seem to smile wide enough. "I'm afraid there isn't much to tell. We didn't do much sightseeing and spent most of our time lying on the sand like two beached whales outside our resort."

"I'm sure you guys found enough to keep you busy." Shelby rolled her eyes.

"Hey." Paige pretended to swat her. "That's your brother's private life you're nosing into."

Shelby held up her hands. "Believe me when I say I don't want to know anything as long as you say you're happy. That's all that matters."

"Incandescently so. Your brother is amazing and I already love being his wife." Paige sipped her iced mocha. "Enough about me. I need to be caught up to speed on your love life."

If Paige had asked her a week ago, Shelby would have squealed with excitement and told her she might be in love with Joel Palermo. Their last time together had been nothing short of a daydream experience. A million times over, she'd replayed in her mind the way he had told her she was worth cherishing, and relived each kiss and tender look. But those memories were always followed by the same question—why hadn't she heard from him since then?

Old fears and the lies she'd believed for so long crowded her thoughts. He'd only pretended not to care about the scars, but really he thought she was disgusting and never wanted to see her again. Joel had done the kind thing, letting her feel loved for a short time, instead of screaming and running away. Knowing how rejection hurt, he'd wanted to spare her feelings so he had simply played along.

Scenarios marched through her thoughts one after another, and for each one, the ending remained the same—Joel didn't want her.

Shelby confessed to Paige the romantic moments she and Joel had shared and the sweet words he had said.

Paige set down her mug. "Wow. So he knows about your scars? You showed him."

"Not by choice. He saw me when I was swimming."

"It sounds like he's a keeper."

"Except he hasn't returned any of my calls, and he hasn't showed up at the building site all week. At first, I thought he must be on shift, but even then he usually stops by. My contractor told me Joel's been stopping by his office every evening to get caught up on the progress, which tells me he's purposely avoiding me." That, and the contractor grumbled about Joel and a police officer nosing around the site. At least he still cared about the church project.

Paige shook her head. "That's not necessarily the case. Remember, he's been through a lot in his life, and it's possible he's afraid to let you down or worried he's not good enough for you, or any number of things. What he needs now, more than ever, is your understanding and compassionate heart. Be patient with him and try not to jump to conclusions until you talk to him."

Shelby traced her fingers over a stain on the table. "It gets harder the more time goes by."

"Don't forget that Caleb and I had our time apart with misunderstandings."

More people were filing into the coffee shop. Soon the tourists would jam the place and fall for the Screaming Joe.

Shelby kept her voice low so nearby tables couldn't overhear. "What if…what if he regrets kissing me? I don't think I can bare that."

"You can ask him right now." Paige waved her arms like she was landing a plane.

Shelby glanced behind her and her breath caught as Joel made his way from the cashier to their table. He wore jeans and a green T-shirt. A man shouldn't be allowed to look that good in something so simple. Or this early in the morning.

Shelby tried to smooth her messed-up-from-the-humidity hair.

Paige vacated her chair and offered it to him. "Here. I was just about to leave."

"That's awful kind of you, Mrs. Beck."

"Ooh!" Paige giggled. "Say that again."

Joel winked. "That was awful kind of you."

"No. The Mrs. Beck part." She swatted his arm. "All right, you two have fun. Caleb will be waking up any minute and probably won't find the note I left saying I was catching coffee with my favorite sister. And his mind will jump to all sorts of horrible places. People are apt to do that when they don't have all the information. Wouldn't you both agree?"

"'Bye, Paige." Shelby gritted her teeth. She loved Paige dearly, but the woman sure knew how to press an issue. Her sister-in-law strolled away from their table and stopped a few times to visit with people before finally exiting the shop.

Joel stood awkwardly by the vacated chair.

Shelby looked up at him. "You don't have to sit there if you don't want to."

"I want to." He crossed his tanned arms over his chest. "I'm just waiting for them to call my name for my coffee."

"Oh."

A moment later, they did, and he went to get his mug. As he sat down across from her, he took a long drink of the liquid, then set his coffee on the table. But he didn't say anything.

Humor always helped to break the ice, right? "Let me guess—you got yourself a Screaming Joe."

He grinned, but it didn't reach his eyes. "I learned

that lesson the hard way. This one is a sissy coffee cara-mel something or other." He sipped again, then set the cup back down. His eyes found hers. "How have you been, Shelb?"

She rubbed her arms. "Good, I guess, but definitely confused."

"About the church?"

She frowned. He knew what she meant. Why make her say it?

"No. I'm good about the church, but where you're concerned I don't know what to think. One moment you're treating me like I'm the best person you've ever met and—"

"That's because you are the best person I've ever met." He stared at the steam drifting off his coffee.

She raised her voice, not caring who heard. "Then why haven't you returned my phone calls?" Everyone within earshot probably thought she was some overat-tached girlfriend. So be it.

Joel leaned forward and spoke softly. "That morn-ing together will go down in my memory as one of the best moments in my entire life."

"Why do I feel like there's a *but* coming?"

"But I don't know the first thing about being a boy-friend. I'm saying this because I care about you so much. You deserve better than me. Caleb was right when he said to steer clear of me because of my past. More right than I could have known."

"That's ridiculous." She snaked her hand across the table to grab his. "I don't know how to be a girlfriend. It's not like I've ever been one. We'll learn together." She let go of his hand and sat back. "Honestly, I'm glad it's about this. I thought you were grossed out about my skin."

"I told you I wasn't. I don't care about your scars. Well, I care. I wish you had never had to go through the pain of having them. That's what I mean."

"Don't worry, I know what you mean. But like I said before, I can't find it in myself to be angry about them anymore because I might not be with you if I didn't have them."

"You definitely wouldn't be."

She sat up straighter. "Excuse me?"

He had the decency to blush. "I mean, if you had been dating, another man would have snatched you up before I ever came back to town."

"I'm glad that didn't happen."

"It's probably not good to be glad about experiencing pain."

"No, you're wrong there. I'm starting to see more and more that God has a bigger plan for our personal pain and suffering. So much bigger than I ever imagined."

His eyes shifted away from hers. "Shelby, have you seen the news about the fire in Colorado?"

"Of course. Why?" How could she miss it? The wildfire had been the first news item on every channel all week.

"I'm thinking of going." He tapped the table twice, almost to convince himself. "That's why I've been quiet all week. I've been deciding if I should volunteer to help."

"Wouldn't it be dangerous?"

"No more dangerous than when I did it before."

But she hadn't known to worry and fear for his safety before. She opened her mouth to speak, but couldn't find the words to tell him not to go. It would be selfish to stop him from serving others.

He fiddled with the handle of his coffee mug. Basically, he did everything except look her in the eye. "If I go, would you be able to watch Dante for me?"

"Of course."

"I need to see Wheeler, then. He wants to talk to me, and I'm assuming he'll be asking if I've made up my mind." He downed the rest of his coffee and stood. "See you later?"

"Definitely." She watched him walk away and tried to feel comforted by their conversation. Of course Joel would be worried about the people in Colorado. They might lose their homes. Their livelihoods. He cared about others. She'd seen this side of his personality many times since he returned to Goose Harbor, and liked him for it.

But she couldn't shake the feeling he was hiding something. Was the fire more dangerous than usual? Could he be concerned she would worry too much? The next time they talked, she'd have to find out the reason for his stilted answers.

Chapter Sixteen

"You wanted to see me, sir?" Joel tapped on the chief's office door. He'd come to the fire station quickly after receiving a message from Wheeler. The conversation with Shelby hadn't been planned, but he was glad it happened the way it did. Well, as glad as a man could be about shooting himself in the foot.

Going to Colorado would be good for him. He'd be on his own again and have time to spend with his thoughts. Get back in touch with the old Joel. Shelby would have time to realize they weren't a good fit for each other. His past loomed like a roadblock. It was either turn around or bust his tires going forward. Tires were expensive so he pulled a U-turn on their relationship. It was the only reasonable option.

Wheeler finished watering a large hibiscus plant sitting on his windowsill before answering Joel. "How many times will I have to tell you not to call me sir?"

"Probably a couple of thousand and then some after that." Joel entered the room.

"Go ahead and close the door and take a seat."

Joel swallowed hard. Most conversations with

Wheeler didn't require a closed door. Certainly, asking if he was going to Colorado wouldn't have called for that. Joel racked his brain for what he'd done wrong in the past week or so. Maybe the chief was going to yell at him because of how he treated Shelby on the dog-bite case. If so, Joel could handle that. He had been unprofessional. A day or two suspension would be appropriate and he'd tell the chief so.

Chief Wheeler rested against the front of his desk. "In the past week, I've noticed you haven't been acting like yourself here at the station. You've been moodier than usual."

The man spoke the truth. While Joel had been wrestling with what to do about Shelby, he had been quieter than usual, which was saying a lot for an introvert like him. "I'm sorry, Chief. I won't let my personal life get in the way of my job again."

"I'm not asking you to pretend to be happy when you're not." Wheeler turned his paperweight around and around in his hand. "I called you in here because I want to know how I can help you. Seeing one of my men struggling doesn't sit well with me. How can I pray for you?"

Yes! Ask God to change the past. Or not have Shelby mad when she learns. Or...

"I prefer to keep my personal life private, if that's all right." Joel tossed his response out quickly because he was afraid he might actually tell Wheeler everything. The chief possessed a welcoming spirit that made a person want to share things with him. But the truth would mean Joel's job. And having arson on his record would ruin any chance he'd have of ever securing a position as a firefighter again.

Wheeler set the paperweight on his desk with a thud. "Son, you've been carrying a burden for a long time. Too long. It's got you tied down and changing yourself just to protect the heavy load. You think no one will care or have your back when you finally talk, but that's where you're wrong. Share it with me so I can help you."

If he wasn't a grown man, Joel might have been tempted to cover his ears and hum. The chief was right. The secret weighed on his soul. Often, he couldn't find words to pray because it seemed like God wouldn't listen to a man with a past like Joel's. Despite the consequences, he wanted to tell someone, especially now that Shelby was involved.

Joel shoved his fingers against his closed eyes. "I burned down the church." He hunched his shoulders and waited for the yelling. Braced himself to be fired on the spot. For Wheeler to not have his back even though he'd just promised he would.

The chief sighed. "I know you did. I've known your secret for a long time."

Joel's head snapped up. Wheeler didn't look shocked or angry. All of his body language—uncrossed arms and legs, his stance leaning slightly toward Joel, open face—told him to keep talking, but Joel couldn't. He'd just shared his darkest secret and received no reaction.

"You can't know I did it." Joel rubbed his palms back and forth over the fabric on his thighs. "No one knows. It's not possible."

Wheeler pursed his lips. "No offense, son, but it didn't take a rocket scientist to figure out who burned down the church. It went up, and hours later, you were reported missing and never seen again. The rest of the town was too wrapped up with the destruction of the church to connect the two, but it sounded like an open-and-shut case to me."

"Are you going to fire me?" Even to his own ears, Joel's voice sounded very small in the closed room.

"Let's see." He scratched his beard. "It wouldn't go well for business if the town discovered we had a fire-fighter who liked to play arson."

Then that was it. He'd lost his job and any life he'd hoped to build here or anywhere. One confession had brought him right back to being that sixteen-year-old boy with no home, no family and no place to go.

Sitting in his chair wouldn't work anymore. His legs needed to move. "It's not like I enjoyed doing it. I was a stupid kid who was mad at God." Joel grabbed the back of his neck, and paced in the small space by the windows. "Why did I even tell you?"

"Because your heart is too good to hold that type of all-consuming secret. You want to be a better man, Joel, I see that about you. But you can't move on until you close this chapter in your life."

Joel stopped pacing and looked out the window. He watched boats leave wakes in the lake. Let his eyes fix on a couple of tourists having fun on a WaveRunner. While they laughed, his life crumbled.

He braced his hands on the shelf full of photographs that ran the length of the windows. "Even if closing that chapter means being arrested for a crime I committed when I was an angry teen?"

Wheeler scooted off his desk and sat in one of the chairs usually reserved for guests. He pointed to the second seat. Joel took the hint and sat back down.

The chief dragged his chair so they faced each other.

"I don't know if you are aware, but I'm the firefighter who rescued Shelby."

Sweat had broken out on the back of Joel's neck and arms. A drop rolled down his shirt. "I wasn't aware."

The chief must despise him, and he had every right to. Joel pictured a younger Wheeler fighting to get into the blaze and then searching all the rooms to see if anyone was inside. The chief would have found Shelby passed out under a burning beam, removed it and carried her to safety. He would have endured seeing her oozing burns, melted skin and charred hair. Perhaps he'd heard her screams and cries when she'd regained consciousness.

The coffee in Joel's stomach rolled.

During training, instructors tried to prepare future firefighters for such sights, but nothing they did could really get a person ready. Especially not when a child was involved. Joel had dry heaved for days after rescuing his first burn victim. And he knew from his own experience that Wheeler must envision Shelby, burned, in his mind over and over.

Joel dropped his head into his hands as tears started to gather. "I'm so sorry. I'm so sorry. You have no idea how much I've regretted starting that fire. I've wished it away a hundred times." He was openly sobbing now. When was the last time he had cried? He'd been a child. Single digits. But he couldn't stop the tears. They choked him and made it hard to speak.

Wheeler laid his hand on Joel's shoulder. "Shelby's become like a daughter to me over the years. I feel a need to protect her. When she was in the hospital, I brought her flowers and held her hand. She's just as much a part of my family as my own children."

Joel wiped his face with the back of his arm. "I understand. I'll never talk to her again. I told her this morning that I'm no good for her."

"But did you tell her you set the fire that changed her life?"

A lump the size of Michigan lodged itself in Joel's throat. He swallowed a few times. "No." He shook his head. "I can't. She'd hate me. How do you tell someone something like that?"

The chief squeezed Joel's shoulder. "Perhaps she'll forgive you, like I have."

"You?" Joel finally looked up from the floor. "Forgive me? How? I can't even forgive myself."

"The day you set that fire you were an angry and scared boy. You wanted a home, and every time you had hope, it was snatched from you. I consider myself a fairly good read of people and I don't think you want to be that frightened boy anymore."

Wheeler stood and made his way to the long shelf running along the large window in his office. Every inch was packed with framed photos of firefighters. Some black-and-white prints. Some full color. A few were group shots that looked like they had been taken twenty years ago.

He selected one in the back and handed it to Joel. The firefighter in the photo wore his blue honor guard uniform. "This is Brandon Moncado. He was twenty-seven when he rushed into a burning apartment building in nearby Brookside. Brandon saved a grandmother and the four toddlers she was babysitting. The building was old. Weak. It crumbled and many people became trapped inside. Including Brandon. He left a wife and a newborn son."

"I'm sorry for your loss," Joel whispered the words automatically, but meant them more than he'd ever meant them before.

"The truth is, I never knew Brandon on this side of life. For the most part, I don't know any of the men on this shelf. But as first responders, they're my brothers and they're here so I can pray for their families like I'd want someone to do for mine should the worst ever happen." He took the photo from Joel and returned it to the shelf. "They're also here to remind me that firefighters are special. When everyone else is running away from danger, we run into it. We don't balk from the hard parts of life, because we know how fragile it can be. Saving Shelby taught me that."

He sat in the chair across from Joel again. "You need to face your mistake head-on. No more hiding. Run at this problem with determination. Fight for the good in this situation. Treat it like a fire that needs to be put out. Do you understand me?"

"I think so." Joel ran his hands through his hair. "But what if the police arrest me?"

"We'll cross that bridge when we get there. Just know that I'm with you in all of this, no matter what happens. All right?"

"Okay." His hands shook. When God brought Joel back to Goose Harbor, Joel thought it was to set down roots in the one place that had always been home. But maybe he needed to return to give everyone in town closure about the fire. "What should I do about Shelby?"

"You need to tell her as soon as possible."

"I will."

Wheeler nodded and then stood. He circled his desk and pulled a folder from a drawer. "I've been talking with some of the hotshot teams, and if you're still willing to volunteer, we can have you on a flight to Colorado today."

"You're not going to suspend me? What about the arson? I didn't think you'd let me work after finding out about that."

"Remember, I knew about it when I hired you. You're a good firefighter and an excellent EMT. The people in Colorado need you and I'll happily send you out there backed by department resources." He pushed the folder across the desk. "Here's the information for the team you're going to meet up with. Your plane ticket is in there, so don't lose that folder." Wheeler eased back into his huge leather chair. "You're free to go."

"Thank you." Joel took the folder and rose to his feet slowly. Should he say something else? He glanced in the folder. The plane left in four hours. That didn't leave him much time to pack his gear and get to the airport.

Wheeler was right about Shelby. Joel needed to tell her about the fire today, before he left. If something happened to him in Colorado…she deserved to hear the truth from him. Everything Caleb said on his wedding day came back to Joel. Dreams were worth chasing and Joel would be a fool to think the pain involved in confessing wouldn't be worth it in the end. Perhaps Shelby wouldn't want anything to do with him, but maybe it would help her heal to know God hadn't hurt her that day. Joel had let her believe that lie for far too long. No more.

He stepped into the hallway.

"Palermo?" Wheeler called after him. "God has the best for you in all of this. Don't you doubt that for one minute. That's an order."

Joel braced his hand on the wall.

Did he believe God cared about his best? *Yes*. For the first time in his life, he did.

Shelby tried to focus on the crew laying the foundation for the church. When she and Joel had first started talking building plans for the church, he had told her the foundation was the most important part. If something compromised it while it was being set, the whole church's structure could weaken over the years. Miles had stopped by earlier—in full police mode—and checked over the contractor's supplies. He'd been doing that a lot lately.

By noon, the thermometer read ninety-six degrees. Who said it could be that hot in Michigan? She pushed up her sleeves a bit, letting her scars show. After speaking with Joel at the coffee shop, she'd decided to trust him and stop hiding under her long sleeves. People could love her as she was or choose not to be her friend. Their loss, right? Well, it helped to tell herself that anyway.

She glanced at her phone and reread Joel's text.

Leaving for Colorado. Can I drop off instructions for Dante?

So he was going.

Her heart rattled in her chest. What if something happened to him? What if he decided to stay in Colorado?

Before she had time to worry any longer she heard the rumble of his motorcycle. The sight of him in his fitted jeans, leather coat and shiny helmet made her heart pound even harder. No matter how long she was bound to know him, remembering that he chose to be with her would make Shelby catch her breath every single time.

He pulled off his helmet and left it on his bike. "Looks like a lot of progress." Joel pointed across the street to the church site.

"Foundation work."

"Important stuff."

"My boyfriend tells me it's the most important." She winked at him.

He looked to his left, out toward the lake. "Sometimes the smallest crack can ruin everything. Of course, big cracks can do a lot more damage right from the start."

She got the feeling he wasn't talking about the church any longer. Maybe he never had been. "Do you have to leave tonight?"

"I'm heading to the airport from here."

"So soon."

He nodded and then pulled handwritten instructions from his coat pocket. "This page has my crew number. If you want updates, watch the news because sometimes they'll reference crew numbers. I won't be able to answer my phone most of the time, so the news is the best way to stay up-to-date. Well, if you want to be."

She unfolded the page and ran her fingers over the number 178. "Of course I'll want to be. Please be safe. I know it's your job, but…" Shelby's voice caught. "I'll miss you so much."

He took her arm and guided her to the end of the block, beside a meadow that would soon become the church parking lot. "I need to tell you something, but I'm afraid to."

Was it about…? She shook the thought away, no longer allowing herself to doubt that Joel was attracted to her despite her scars. "You can tell me anything. I trust you."

He turned to the side so she could see only his profile. "Don't say that."

The pain laced in his voice caused fear to skitter down her back. "Joel, what's going on?"

"I love you."

Her lips instantly tugged into a smile and she took a deep breath. The summer air, perfumed with flowers, smelled sweeter than usual. No one had ever said those three words to her in a romantic way. She didn't want to ruin the moment, but needed to say something because he looked so worried.

She laid her hand on his arm. "That's not something to be afraid of."

Joel faced her. "That's not all I need to tell you. See, I wanted to say I love you before I tell you the other thing. You need to know how I feel in case I never get the opportunity to talk to you again."

"You're scaring me. Please, just tell me whatever you need to."

"I'm the one who set the fire. The church. I burned it down."

Shelby stumbled backward as if she'd been struck. Her lungs closed in. She couldn't take a breath deep enough to give her brain sufficient oxygen. Black spots darted into her vision.

Not again.

After the fire, she'd suffered from panic attacks, but it had been years since she'd had one. Only every once in a while, when she woke from a vivid nightmare of being stuck under the beam, did she experience an attack.

Nightmares about a fire that Joel had set.

He cupped her elbows and caught her when her knees buckled. "Shelb. Please say something. Do you need help? An ambulance?"

Be strong. She'd faced the worst in life and come out the other end. She could face the man who had caused all her pain without passing out. She had to.

Shelby shoved him away. "Don't touch me. I don't want you to touch me ever again."

"Shelby—"

Ramming her finger into his chest, she allowed the ball of rage bubbling inside of her to fuel her words. "You ruined my life. You could have killed me. Is that what you wanted? Did you think it was funny?"

"No. Please." He reached for her, but she moved back. "I looked in the windows and didn't see anyone. I would have never... I'm so sorry."

"I don't want to hear it."

"Shelb—"

"Stop! Don't say my name. I don't want to talk to you again." She knew she should hear him out, but couldn't stomach it. The pain from years of hiding and being held back in life spilled out of her. All the anger she'd held behind the dutiful smile of a loving sister and happy neighbor had found a target. And the bull's-eye had a name and a face now. If she heaped her pain on Joel and blamed him for all the wrongs she'd experienced, then maybe she'd finally be free of it all.

"Whatever you say." He trudged back to his motorcycle and started to unfasten his helmet.

Unable to restrain herself, she followed him. "I'll still watch Dante because it's not his fault you're his owner. But I don't need your help on the church any-more. You're the last person who should be involved."

His shoulders fell as he faced her. "Did you ever ac-tually care about me or was I just another hurt dog for you to take care of?"

The look in his eyes made her chest sting. Joel had been pitied and abandoned his entire life. Even though she was upset with him, it took all the strength she had left to fight her desire to comfort him. "Don't you dare make this about yourself! Honestly, I have no more words for you."

"Then I won't take up any more of your time. God bless you, Shelby. I messed up a good chunk of your life, but I hope you know you deserve the best."

She turned away to hide her tears. Why did it have to hurt so much? She had cared for Joel—still did, if she was being honest. But how could they move forward with something like the fire between them?

His motorcycle rumbled. The engine's vibrations shook her body as he kicked it into gear and roared off. Long after she could no longer hear Joel's bike, she stayed rooted in the same spot, tears streaming down her cheeks, ears straining to hear him return.

Chapter Seventeen

Maybe Shelby had changed her mind.

When the plane touched down in Colorado, Joel checked his messages. Zero. Zip. Nothing. So much for wishful thinking.

He grabbed his gear and found a man named Benny who had been sent to pick him up and bring him to the base site. Benny was a man of great beard and few words. An hour into their drive, thick black smoke began to cover the sky. After serving two years on hotshot teams, Joel knew the sight well and braced himself for the adrenaline rush that would come from charging into fires hundreds of miles long. Benny told him his crew would be heading out that evening.

Joel's phone vibrated in his pocket. *Shelby?* A man could hope. But he didn't recognize the number. "Hello?"

"Joel? This is Miles." He cleared his throat. "Officer Reid."

"How can I help you?" Joel tried to keep his voice even so Benny wouldn't know something was wrong.

The smoke in the air now blocked out the sun.

"Chief Wheeler stopped by the police department today and told me you confessed to the church arson." Miles paused. "Is that true?"

He could lie. Say Wheeler was out of his mind. Make up some story about it being a big joke. But then he wouldn't be trusting that the situation could be worked out in a way that would bring glory to God.

Joel propped his elbow against the window. "It's true."

"I'll need the confession in writing from you. It'll be nice to finally close this case."

Benny turned the vehicle off the road and rolled down his window to talk to policemen stationed at a barricade. When they ducked to glance in the car, Joel felt like they could see his guilt, but they flagged the car through.

"I'm not in town right now."

"Wheeler told me as much, but I'll need to see you at the station when you're back in town."

To make an arrest?

Joel worked his jaw back and forth. He wanted to ask the question but didn't want Benny to overhear. If the man discovered Joel was under investigation for a crime, he would strike him from the list of approved hotshots right away. Even if it hadn't been arson... The fact that it *was* merely solidified his need to end the conversation with Miles.

"I'll let you know when I'm back in town."

"Joel?"

"Yes?"

"A lot of people wouldn't have come forward for something like this. It shows you're a man of character."

"Thanks, Miles."

"Be safe out there."

"See you soon."

That evening, as he tried to sleep on the hard concrete of a closed-off road with the rest of crew 178, Joel had a difficult time closing his eyes. Whenever he did, he saw Shelby's face—cheeks red with anger and eyes flat as she'd shoved him away from her, telling him she never wanted to see him again.

Maybe it was for the best. No, he was just telling himself that. He loved Shelby and wanted to be with her. During the entire flight to Colorado he'd prayed they could one day bridge all that separated them and become the answer to her prayer from fourteen years ago—a husband and wife who loved each other, and parents who would be there for their children. They could be the ones to change the legacy of their families if they were willing to put in a lot of hard work, have mountains of grace for each other and allow God free rein to work in their lives.

It could happen. Maybe.

He rolled onto his side, but it didn't help. Firefighters slept on the roads for safety reasons. If the wind changed directions, the wildfire could move rapidly and unexpectedly. Concrete and asphalt didn't start on fire instantly. If the wildfire changed course and came at the crew, being on the street would give them a couple of extra minutes to get to a safer place.

Turning onto his back again, he tried to make out the constellations, but smoke blotted out most of the stars' light. The air smelled like chemicals, more than likely a mixture of the buildings and personal belongs being swallowed by the fire. People's dreams gone in seconds.

But he wasn't about to let another fire steal something so important to him.

God, be with Shelby. Take care of her. Help bring healing to her life and show her she is loved just as she is.

"He's going to be all right." Paige handed Shelby an iced tea as she sank onto the plush sofa beside her.

It hadn't taken Shelby long to cool off from her fight with Joel. Unleashing years of hurt might have felt relieving in the moment, but it had been the wrong thing to do. Joel wasn't the enemy—not really. A few days apart, a talk with Chief Wheeler and time spent praying had shown her that.

Shelby kept her eyes on the television screen. She'd been so wrapped up in the church rebuild the past few weeks that she hadn't realized how huge the Colorado wildfire had become. The blaze had gobbled up acres and acres of forest. Why hadn't she paid attention when Joel had first brought it up?

The church rebuild had stalled. It was still under way, but she was letting Chief Wheeler and Miles handle the details. They were better at keeping the contractor in line anyway.

Besides, she didn't need to see the church in one piece to feel whole again. That had always been the wrong way to think about her situation. Her healing hadn't ever been tied to the church, but to her own stubborn heart. She'd slammed the door on all opportunities God had brought into her life, which could have led to healing. It wasn't Joel's fault, or her father's or anyone else she'd blamed along the way.

Only hers.

What a wake-up call.

While she still cared about the church rebuild, her attention had become focused on wanting Joel home safe and sound.

Since Joel had left Goose Harbor, she'd spent most of every day holed up in his house with Dante. But being there kept him on her mind constantly so she'd talked Caleb and Paige into letting her and Dante come to their house in the evenings for company.

Shelby sipped the iced tea but couldn't have told someone what it tasted like. Her focus was squarely on the television. Why were they talking about baseball scores when the fire still raged?

The front door to the house burst open and Caleb charged in. He stopped and looked both of the women over. "You don't know, do you?" He sounded out of breath.

Paige laid her hand on Shelby's knee. "Don't know what?"

Bold letters reading Crew 178 now flashed on the screen.

He snatched the remote off the coffee table and unmuted the television. "Joel's crew is—"

"Shh!" Shelby jumped to her feet.

The overly tanned reporter pulled a grim face. "…reported to be trapped in the middle of the wildfire." A map filled the screen. Animated orange blazes covered town names she'd never heard of, but right in the middle of all the orange was a white circle with the number 178 written inside. "As of this moment, it's uncertain if the men will be reached in time."

Shelby dropped back into her seat. "No. No. No. This can't be happening."

Caleb rushed to her side. "Let's pray for him. Right now." He grabbed Shelby's hand and reached for Paige's. "Father God, right now we're worried about our friend Joel. Keep him safe, Lord. Bring him home to us. Let him complete the work You've set for him to do on this earth. And, God, please heal Shelby's pain. She's hurting knowing that the man she cares about is the one who gave her the scars she's been hiding for so long. Show Your hand in all of this. We ask these things in Your Son's powerful name. Amen."

"Amen." Paige squeezed her hand.

"Amen." Shelby kept her eyes closed and heard Joel's voice in her head.

People hurt other people—whether we mean to or not. I'll try my hardest to never cause you pain, and someday when I do, I'll do everything in my power to make it right.

What right did she have to expect him to be perfect? Relationships—even good ones—involved confusion and discomfort and, yes, pain at some point.

She kept hold of Caleb's hand and opened her eyes slowly. "What if he dies?"

Caleb hooked his free hand on the back of his neck. "You can't think like that right now."

"I should have forgiven him when I had the chance. He told me he was walking into a dangerous situation and I told him I never wanted to see him again. Why didn't I tell him I forgave him? I don't want to lose him." She scrubbed her hand across her eyes. The past two months had caused her to cry more than the past ten years combined. In a good way. Shelby was living again—feeling things again. All thanks to Joel.

Paige moved to sit on the coffee table so the three

of them could form a huddle. "You've been through so much. It's okay that you reacted the way you did."

Shelby stood and brushed past Paige. She needed room to move. "But it's not okay. I've been using that fire as a crutch for so many things in my life." She yanked her phone out of her back pocket. "Joel doesn't have control over something that happened fourteen years ago and he never meant to hurt me. The fact is, I'm in love with him. I was so stupid not to tell him."

Caleb pointed to her phone. "Then go ahead and tell him now."

Shelby spent the next two hours hitting redial and getting voice mail. Listening to his voice repeat his message again and again calmed her. When he finally saw all his missed calls from her number he would probably think she was insane, but that would be okay because to have that thought meant he'd be alive.

On the last call, she decided to leave a message. "This is Shelby. I want you to know that I forgive you and I miss you like crazy. When you get this message, hurry home to me, okay? Forget everything I said the last time we talked. We're all praying for you."

Caleb and Paige took over the couch and Shelby snagged the small love seat. They turned the channel to one of the twenty-four-hour news networks. Shelby asked to borrow Caleb's laptop and kept refreshing the screen for the most current information on the fire.

It kept hitting her how many people were losing their entire lives. People were missing. Families were looking for relatives. Entire communities were gone.

She couldn't help Joel at the moment, but she could join him in helping the people in the midst of the wildfire. Sure, she wasn't tangibly there, but she could spend all night praying for the families affected, for rescue personnel, for protection for the missing people, for rain to fall and for Joel's safety.

Finally closing the laptop, she glanced at Caleb and Paige, who had fallen asleep leaning on each other. Shelby yawned and reached by her feet to pet Dante, but she touched carpeting. Odd. The dog usually stuck close by.

She got to her feet and stretched. "Dante," she whispered, which was silly because the dog was half-deaf.

After searching the entire lower level of the house, she was wide-awake and starting to panic.

"Dante!" She no longer cared if she woke up her brother and his wife. There was no reason for the dog to have gone upstairs. He had arthritis in his legs and the stairs would have hurt him. But she dashed up the steps two at a time and scoured the bedrooms for him.

Her heart lodged in her throat and pounded an uneven beat against her temples. She rushed into the living room and found Caleb and Paige rubbing their faces and stretching. "Have either of you seen Dante?"

"Yeah." Paige yawned. "He was whining at the door, so I let him out back a while ago."

Caleb's jaw dropped. "Paige…the back gate is broken."

Shelby raced her brother to the back door. She flung it open and charged outside. "Dante! Here, pup. Where are you, boy?"

But Dante was gone.

Chapter Eighteen

"Shelby." Someone jiggled her shoulder.

She jolted awake. "Did you find Dante?" She latched on to Paige's arm.

Shelby blinked, and Joel's living room came into focus—a small room, bare except for a very well-used plaid couch she lay on and an old television with rabbit ears that sat on a milk crate. Nothing else. She'd insisted on going back to Joel's modest rental home after the search finished each night in case Dante decided to return to the place he knew.

Paige patted her hand. "No. But I talked to Wheeler and he's been in touch with the hotshot center in Colorado. Joel should be headed back home today."

"I was so scared for him. What would I have done if his crew hadn't been rescued?"

When Shelby had stopped by Joel's house for the first time almost two months ago, she'd figured he was still waiting for boxes of his belongings to arrive, but no more possessions ever showed up. The house had a single bedroom across from the bathroom. He'd left the door open once and she'd found only a mattress on the floor and a duffel bag of clothing.

The one photograph in the entire house was fixed to the fridge with a magnet. It showed Joel hugging a younger Dante.

Joel had no home. No family. No roots. Nothing besides Dante.

She'd known those things were true, but the gravity of the situation hadn't struck her until she stood in his house this morning. Sickness crept up her throat. How would she explain everything to Joel if and when he returned to Goose Harbor?

Shelby pointed to Paige's arm where her sister-in-law always kept an assortment of hair ties. "Can I borrow one?"

"Sure." Paige handed her a blue tie.

Pulling up her hair, Shelby made her way to the bathroom. She grabbed the mouthwash sitting on the counter and swished. Bags under her eyes and cracked lips told the story of her past two days. Her feet hurt, too. If Joel had left his truck, she would have used it in the search instead of going by foot or waiting for other people to drive her. But Joel must have swapped out his motorcycle for his truck after he'd seen her the last time because she'd found his bike in the driveway.

Shelby returned to the living room and pulled on her shoes. "I'm going out to look for him again."

Paige blocked the doorway. "It's been two days."

"And we haven't found him yet." Shelby inched around Paige.

But she stepped in front of her again. "You were up all night searching for him and spent all day yesterday making more flyers and contacting every police department in a twenty-mile radius."

"There aren't that many." Shelby crossed her arms. She would push her scrawny sister-in-law out of the way if she had to. "Don't you get it? That dog is the only family he's got. I have to find Dante before Joel gets back."

"Caleb and Miles are out looking right now. Why don't you wait until they return?"

"Because I'm not going to sit around and relax until he's found." Shelby brushed past Paige and laid her hand on the front-door knob. "What if...what if I have to tell Joel that I lost his dog? He could react the same way I did when he told me about the fire. I didn't mean to lose Dante any more than he meant to trap me in a burning building. But he could be angry. He could decide we shouldn't be together after this."

"Right now, you have to trust that he's not going to react that way."

Shelby looked out the small window of the door and saw Joel's truck roll up the driveway. "He's home." She breathed.

She'd misplaced her phone at Caleb's house the other night and Paige had returned it today with a dead battery. If Joel had tried to call her, she wouldn't know. It was possible he'd never listened to her message saying she forgave him. All she knew was that he was alive. And home. And only twenty feet outside the house where she stood.

She ripped open the door and ran down the front walk. Joel had just closed the driver's door when she barreled into him. Shelby threw her arms around him.

"You're safe! Wheeler said you were, but I couldn't breathe right until I saw you…I'm so happy." First she kissed one side of his face and then the other side.

"Shelb—"

She stopped his words with a kiss and wove her hands into his smooth hair. He needed a shower, but she couldn't have cared less. Joel dropped the bag he'd been holding and pressed his hands into the small of her back to bring her flush against his chest.

After they parted, he still held her close. He pressed his nose into her hair and breathed once deeply. Then he rested his forehead against hers. "That's the best welcome home I'll probably ever get."

"I'll do that every day if you let me."

"Why, Shelby Beck." He took her shoulder and set her a foot away to study her face. "Are my ears playing tricks or did you just ask me to marry you in a back-door kind of way?" His voice told her he was teasing. Joel must have received her voice mail.

Hooking her hands into his coat pockets, she pulled him close again. "I'm saying I'm in love with you. That's what."

"I love you, too. But you knew that already."

If she could have stayed in this moment, she would have, but Caleb's heavy footsteps up the driveway made reality crash in. They couldn't stay like this, because she had to fess up about Dante.

"Joel, I have to tell you something." She grabbed his hand.

Paige opened the front door and came on to the stoop. Joel glanced at Paige, then Caleb and then Miles as he walked up the sidewalk toward them.

Miles tucked a walkie-talkie into a clip on his belt. "No sign of him."

Joel's eyebrows shot up. "No sign of who?" He locked gazes with Shelby. "Can someone tell me why there are so many people at my house at nine in the morning on a Thursday?"

Say it. Quick. Like ripping off a bandage.

"Dante's missing."

"Missing?" Joel dropped her hand and looked around at everyone. "I don't understand."

"I lost him. I'm so sorry." Shelby stared at the tips of her tennis shoes. "I understand if you're angry at me."

She waited for him to say something. Braced her muscles for him to yell or tell her to leave.

Joel watched Shelby. Her face fell and her shoulders drooped, then straightened as if she was trying to be strong.

Dante was gone.

Joel swallowed hard. Dante was his best friend. He couldn't let him wander around homeless, get hurt or think Joel had abandoned him.

"How long has he been missing?"

"Two days." She kept her gaze glued to the ground.

Too long. The information sunk like a lead weight in his stomach. Dante could be anywhere by now. Something terrible could have happened to him. They should have tried harder to find him. They should have...

God grant patience and grace.

Using two of his fingers, he tipped up Shelby's chin so her eyes met his. Red lines in her eyes and deep bags under them spoke of sleepless nights. Shelby hadn't lost

Dante on purpose. She loved dogs and wouldn't want anything bad to happen to his. Knowing her like Joel did, she had been going out of her mind with worry.

He took her hand, laced his fingers with hers. "Let's go find him."

He turned to Caleb, Paige and Miles. "You guys have checked all the animal shelters?"

Caleb nodded. "No sign of him."

Miles hooked his hands on his work belt. "They'll contact you if he's found. That's why dogs in Michigan have to be licensed. Then all their information is on file if they're lost."

Joel tightened his hold on Shelby. "That's great, except that I've been so busy since moving here that I haven't gotten Dante his license yet."

Miles's face fell. "Oh. Then we should all contact the shelters and leave your information in case he's found."

Caleb grabbed Paige's hand. "We'll walk the shoreline again. Shelby says Dante loves the water."

Joel nodded. "And Shelby and I will expand the search to other towns."

Shelby hopped into the truck and Joel turned to join her, but Miles caught his arm. Would he arrest him now? In front of Shelby? Surely Miles would wait until they found Dante.

Joel handed Shelby his cell. "Start calling shelters. I'll be back in a second."

He motioned for Miles to walk with him on the sidewalk. "I'm assuming you want to talk to me about the arson. I know I said I'd go straight to the police department when I returned, and I will once we find Dante. I promise. Let me just—"

Miles smiled and it covered half his face. Did police officers get a sick pleasure out of arresting their childhood friends? "I talked to the prosecutor's office. We won't be pressing charges."

In the rush to go to Colorado and while fighting the fire, Joel hadn't had the time or energy to research his rights as far as arson laws in Michigan.

Joel ran his fingers over the stubble on his jaw. "Not pressing charges... I'm just a simple fireman who doesn't get police talk. Does that mean I'm not going to be arrested?"

Miles nodded.

A knot undid itself in Joel's chest. He could breathe again. No more tightness.

"But I confessed. You can't get better proof than that."

"It turns out you're long past the statute of limitations for arson in our state."

Joel grabbed Miles and gave him a quick back-thumping hug. First, Shelby had said she loved him, and now Miles was telling him the arson wasn't going to ruin his life. If they found Dante, this would be the best day of his life. Easy.

Miles grabbed Joel by the shoulders. "You'll still have to come to the station and provide a written statement so I can close the case, but that'll be the end of it."

"Thank you."

"I didn't do anything."

"You're treating me like a friend and not like a horrible person who got away with a crime."

"That's because we *are* friends. But I am going to have to ticket you for not having Dante licensed."

"I deserve it."

"We can do that later, though. For now let's stop yapping and find your dog." Miles promised to have all the officers keep an eye out for Dante.

Joel climbed back into the truck and turned off the radio when the truck started so Shelby could hear while she talked on the phone. He drove slowly around the town square.

"So, you haven't seen a dog like that?" Shelby asked, gripping his cell. "Okay. Can I give you our number to call us if you do find him?"

After she hung up, Shelby filled him in on where they'd searched. "We've turned over every rock in Goose Harbor and Shadowbend. I made flyers and put them up everywhere. There's even a reward."

"Shelby." Joel squeezed her hand. "I appreciate all you've done, but I know you don't have a ton of money right now. You didn't have to offer a reward."

"It's Caleb's money."

"I'll double whatever is listed on the poster."

"I'm so sorry about this. I should have—"

"Hey." He smiled at her. "You didn't do it on purpose. I have faith we'll find him."

"Joel, I know you didn't know I was in the church when you lit it on fire." She paused. "I'm sorry I treated you so horribly when you told me."

He didn't know what had made her say that, but another knot in his chest unwound at her words.

Joel shrugged. "I deserved it. At the time, I knew starting the church on fire was a sin and I still chose to do wrong."

"None of that matters anymore. Okay? I forgive you."

"Thank you."

Shelby dialed the number to a forest preserve on the off chance that a ranger had spotted Dante.

Two phone calls later and Joel's heart sank into the bottom of his shoes. He had to face the possibility that Dante was gone for good. After Shelby's next call, he'd take her back to her apartment so she could nap. He couldn't mourn the loss of his friend in front of her. That would only make her feel worse.

Shelby braced her hand on the dashboard. "Yes. He's an Australian cattle dog. Older. Right." She paused. "Don't do anything. Please. We'll be there in an hour." She dropped the phone into the cup holder. "We found him."

Joel rolled down the window and whooped to let out pent-up energy.

Shelby laughed. "Let's go get your buddy."

He handed her the GPS unit. "Lead the way."

Shelby let go of Joel's hand as they walked through the cat room of the Quiet Oaks Pet Shelter. At least thirty cats milled around the room. She'd never been a huge fan of cats, but it bothered her that so many felines couldn't find a home.

The shelter worker, Connie, pointed to all the black cats. "They're harder to find homes for. Many people believe black cats are mean or bad luck. In America, more black cats are put down than any other color of cat."

"That's so sad." Shelby scratched behind a black cat's ears before they left the room. He purred and followed her until Connie closed the door. "All because of how they look?"

"I'm afraid so." Connie opened the door to the dog area. They walked past rows and rows of dogs in bare cement-floor cages all waiting for their forever homes. Shelby's heart twisted for every single one of them.

Connie used her swipe pass to get into a room near the back. "I'm hoping this guy in here is yours. He was dropped off two nights ago. A trucker found him at a gas station near the highway and worried he'd get hit. He's an old boy and doesn't hear well. If he's not yours, you may want to think about taking him. We're so over-crowded right now that he's set to be euthanized when the vet stops in at noon."

Shelby gasped and Joel motioned for Connie to open the door. She had only moved it an inch before Dante bounded out. The dog launched himself into Joel's arms, all happy wiggles and flying fur.

"Boy, am I glad to see you." Joel hugged Dante to his neck.

Shelby glanced at the clock on the wall. Eleven. One more hour and they would have put Dante to sleep. Just assumed that no one wanted an old, deaf dog. How many animals met that fate every day? Her stomach turned.

Joel clipped the leash he'd brought to Dante's collar and promised Connie he'd get ID tags and his state license right away. He loaded Dante into the front of the truck and then turned and pulled Shelby in for a hug. "This is the single best day of my life."

"Best?" She laid her hands on his chest so she could look him in the eyes. "Did you hear that woman? They almost killed Dante."

"But they didn't."

"By an hour."

"God got us here on time."

"Still. Dante getting lost shouldn't have happened."

Joel tucked a wayward hair behind Shelby's ear. "We can never change the past. You and I both know that better than anyone. All we can do is learn from it and show grace to others whenever we have the chance."

Shelby climbed into the cab beside Dante, who waited for Joel and then rested his head on his leg. Dante let out a long, happy sigh. With her hand in the dog's fur, Shelby called the rest of the search party and told them the good news.

Joel laid one of his hands over Shelby's and they drove in silence. Almost like a happy little family for the first half of the ride home. But Shelby couldn't shake the thought that if they'd been delayed another hour, or had called the shelters in a different order, Dante would be dead. The information Connie had shared about the black cats bothered her, too. Animals shouldn't face death because people weren't comfortable with how they looked or believed some misinformation about them.

An idea hit her. She tugged her hand out from under Joel's and braced it on the dashboard. "I finally know what I want to do. With my life. For the future."

Joel rested his arm on the back of the seat and ran his fingers over the end of her pony tail. "I'd love to hear about it."

"I don't know how I'll find the money, but I'm going to start a nonkill animal shelter in Goose Harbor. We'll take older animals and unwanted ones that are hard to place and find them forever homes. My slogan will be something like Find Home at Last. I mean, I came up with that off the top of my head. But anything along those lines would work." She peeked over at Joel who grinned from ear to ear. "What do you think? Be honest."

"I think it's the perfect fit for you."

"So let's start brainstorming ways I can come up with the money."

"How about this time around I'll just float you the cash."

"Um. I don't think you comprehend how much an operation like that would take to get off the ground."

She would need land, a building, supplies and insurance to start. It had to be in the six figures dollar-wise merely to get off the ground, and Joel was a man with few possessions and a hole in the floorboard of his truck.

Joel traced the back of her neck. "Believe me. I know what I'm promising. If you haven't noticed by now, I live pretty meagerly and have for the past ten years that I've been working full-time. There's a pretty good stockpile in my back account."

"I can't take your money."

"Shelby, listen to me. I couldn't care less about material things. All I've ever wanted was someone to love who loves me back, and I have that now. I don't need the money. It's just sitting there. It would make me ten times happier to see you pursue your dream than let interest keep gathering."

"If you're sure."

"I'm sure." He reached for her, laced his fingers with hers and then kissed the back of her hand. "This—" he kissed it again "—is all I need. Just don't let go."

"I never will." She tightened her hold and hoped he understood she meant forever.

They spent the rest of the day dreaming up plans for her animal shelter, and in between planning, they snuck in a kiss or two—or five—just to make sure they were making good on their earlier promise to enjoy the present as much as they could.

* * * * *

Dear Reader,

Sometimes life is hard. There's no other way to put it. During the times when life hurts, we often find ourselves asking: *Where's God in the midst of this?*

Joel and Shelby both had things happen to them that they had no control over—like Joel being abandoned by his mother and growing up in the foster system, and Shelby getting burned in the church fire. On the other hand, both of them made poor choices in their lives that also caused problems. Joel committed arson, ran away and tried to hide his past. Shelby swallowed her dreams and pushed people away so she wouldn't have to face the possibility of rejection.

The fact is, we all have scars and we all want to be loved as is. Living a full life requires opening up and being vulnerable to others—which can be scary—but it's worth it in the end. Above all, we can take comfort knowing that God has always loved us just as we are—even before we were willing to love and accept ourselves.

I hope you enjoyed visiting Goose Harbor and getting to know Joel and Shelby. Please come back often and learn what happens to your favorite characters in future books. You can find out more about the Goose Harbor series and see all of my books by visiting www.jessicakellerbooks.com.

Dream Big,

Jess Keller

COMING NEXT MONTH FROM
Love Inspired®

Available February 17, 2015

A WIFE FOR JACOB
Lancaster County Weddings • by Rebecca Kertz

Jacob Lapp has loved Annie Zook since they were twelve years old.
Now that he's working at her father's blacksmith shop, will he finally get
the chance to forge their futures together?

THE COWBOY'S FOREVER FAMILY
Cowboy Country • by Deb Kastner

Rodeo rider Slade McKenna wants to protect his best friend's widow and
baby. As he helps the resilient single mom settle in on her ranch, he'll soon
get his own chance at family.

THE FOREST RANGER'S RESCUE
by Leigh Bale

Forest ranger Brent Knowles begins to fall for the teacher he's hired to
help his young daughter speak again. Can he reconcile his feelings when
his investigation into a forest theft threatens her family's livelihood?

FINDING HIS WAY HOME
Barrett's Mill • by Mia Ross

When prodigal son Scott Barrett returns home, he promises to stay out of
trouble. But soon he's in danger of losing his heart to the beautiful artist
he's helping restore the town's chapel.

ALASKAN HOMECOMING
by Teri Wilson

Returning home, ballerina Posy Sutton agrees to teach dance to the local
girls. When she discovers her boss is old sweetheart Liam Blake, can she
make room in her future for a love from her past?

ENGAGED TO THE SINGLE MOM
by Lee Tobin McClain

Pretending an engagement with ex-fiancé Troy Hinton to fulfill
her ill son's wishes for a daddy, single mom Angelica Camden finds
nothing but complications when she falls head over heels for the
handsome dog rescuer—again!

---

*A young Amish woman yearns for true love.
Read on for a preview of A WIFE FOR JACOB
by Rebecca Kertz, the next book in her
LANCASTER COUNTY WEDDINGS series.*

Annie stood by the dessert table when she saw Jedidiah Lapp chatting with his wife, Sarah. She'd been heartbroken when Jed had broken up with her, and then married Sarah Mast.

Seeing the two of them together was a reminder of what she didn't have. Annie wanted a husband—and a family. But how could she marry when no one showed an interest in her? She blinked back tears. She'd work hard to be a wife a husband would appreciate. She wanted children, to hold a baby in her arms, a child to nurture and love.

She sniffled, looked down and straightened the dessert table. And the pitchers and jugs of iced tea and lemonade.

"May I have some lemonade?" a deep, familiar voice said.

Annie looked up. "Jacob." His expression was serious as he studied her. She glanced down and noticed the fine dusting of corn residue on his dark jacket. "Lemonade?" she echoed self-consciously.

"*Ja*. Lemonade," he said with amusement.

She quickly reached for the pitcher. She poured his lemonade into a plastic cup, only chancing a glance at him when she handed him his drink.

"How is the work going?" she asked conversationally.

"We are nearly finished with the corn. We'll be cutting hay next." He lifted the glass to his lips and took a swallow.

Warmth pooled in her stomach as she watched the movement of his throat. "How's *Dat?*" she asked. She had seen him chatting with her father earlier.

Jacob glanced toward her *dat* with a small smile. "He says he's not tired. He claims he's enjoying the view too much." His smile dissipated. "No doubt he'll be exhausted later."

Annie agreed. "I'll check on him in a while." She hesitated. "Are you hungry? I can fix you a plate—"

He gazed at her for several heartbeats with his striking golden eyes. "*Ne,* I'll fix one myself." He finished his drink and held out his glass to her. "May I?"

She hurried to refill his glass. With a crooked smile and a nod of thanks, Jacob accepted the refill and left. The warm flutter in her stomach grew stronger as she watched him walk away, stopping briefly to chat with Noah and Rachel, his brother and sister-in-law.

Annie glanced over where several men were being dished up plates of food. She then caught sight of Jacob walking along with his brother Eli. The contrast of Jacob's dark hair and Eli's light locks struck her as they disappeared into the barn. They came out a few minutes later, Eli carrying tools, Jacob leading one of her father's workhorses.

As if he sensed her regard, Jacob looked over and locked gazes with her.

Will Annie ever find the husband of her heart?
Pick up A WIFE FOR JACOB to find out.
Available March 2015,
wherever Love Inspired® books and ebooks are sold.

Love the Love Inspired book you just read?

Your opinion matters.

Review this book on your favorite book site, review site, blog or your own social media properties and share your opinion with other readers!